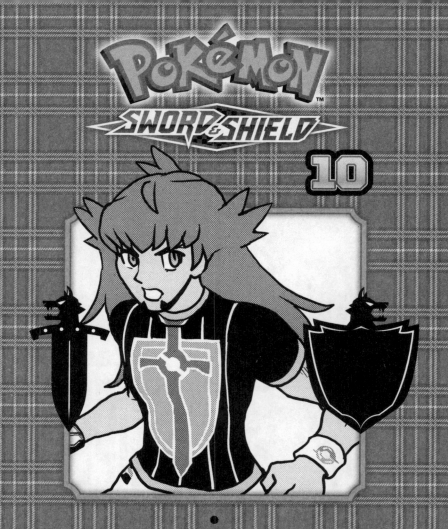

Pokémon

SWORD & SHIELD

10

STORY
Hidenori Kusaka

ART
Satoshi Yamamoto

Henry
SWORD

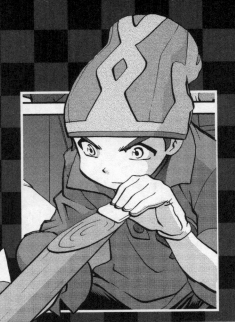

THE DESCENDANT OF A
RENOWNED SWORDSMITH,
HENRY IS AN ARTISAN WHO
FIXES AND IMPROVES
POKÉMON GEAR.

Casey
SHIELD

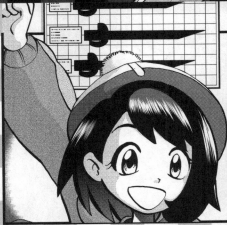

AN ELITE HACKER AND COMPUTER
TECH WHO CAN ACCESS ANY DATA SHE
WANTS. SHE'S PROFESSOR MAGNOLIA'S
ASSISTANT AND IS THE TEAM ANALYST.

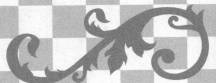

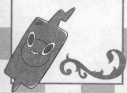

The Story So Far

UPON ARRIVING IN THE GALAR REGION, MARVIN SEES A DYNAMAXED POKÉMON AND FALLS OFF A CLIFF! HE IS SAVED BY HENRY SWORD AND CASEY SHIELD AND JOINS THEM ON THEIR JOURNEY TO COMPLETE THEIR GYM CHALLENGE AND DISCOVER THE SECRET OF DYNAMAXING WITH PROFESSOR MAGNOLIA. RECENTLY, TWO STRANGE TRAINERS APPEARED. THEY SEEM TO HAVE A CONNECTION WITH CHAIRMAN ROSE, BUT WHAT COULD THEY BE AFTER? AND WHAT WILL HAPPEN WHEN THE DARKEST DAY IS UNLEASHED UPON GALAR?!

Marvin

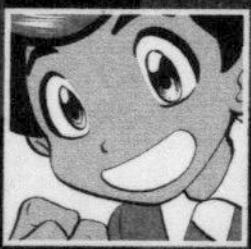

A ROOKIE TRAINER WHO MOVED TO GALAR. HE WORKS WITH HENRY TO LEARN ABOUT THE REGION.

Professor Magnolia

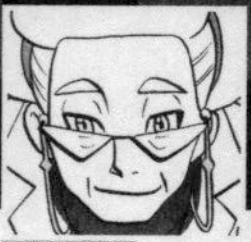

A FAMED RESEARCHER WHO STUDIES "DYNAMAXING," A.K.A. THE GIGANTIFICATION OF POKÉMON. SHE IS A GENTLE SOUL WHO IS FOND OF DRINKING TEA.

Leon

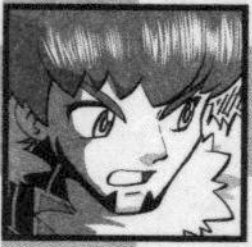

LEON IS THE BEST TRAINER IN GALAR. HE'S THE UNDEFEATED CHAMPION!

Sonia

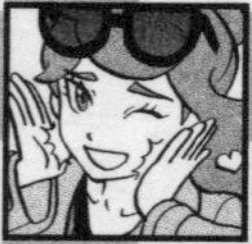

PROFESSOR MAGNOLIA'S GRANDDAUGHTER AND LEON'S CHILDHOOD FRIEND. SHE'S BEEN RESEARCHING THE GALAR LEGEND.

Hop

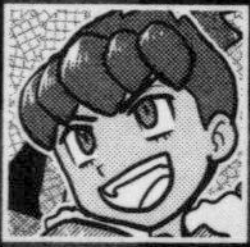

LEON'S YOUNGER BROTHER. HE RESPECTS HIS STRONG BROTHER AND TAKES PART IN THE GYM CHALLENGE.

Bede

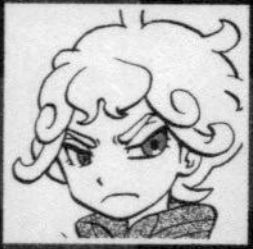

A DISQUALIFIED GYM CHALLENGER WHO WAS LATER RECRUITED TO BE A GYM LEADER.

Sordward & Shielbert

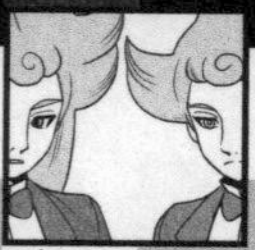

STRANGE BROTHERS WHO ARE ENEMIES OF HENRY AND HIS FRIENDS. THEY CLAIM TO BE DESCENDANTS OF ROYALTY AND HAVE LAUNCHED AN ATTACK!

Rose

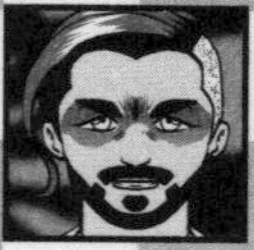

THE CHAIRMAN OF THE POKÉMON LEAGUE AND PRESIDENT OF MACRO COSMOS. HE HAS A DIABOLICAL SCHEME UP HIS SLEEVE!

CONTENTS

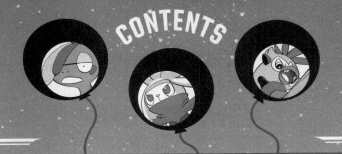

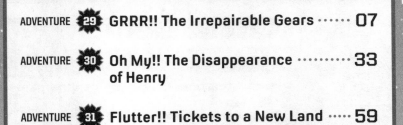
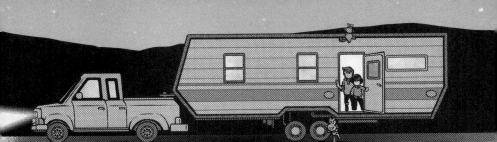

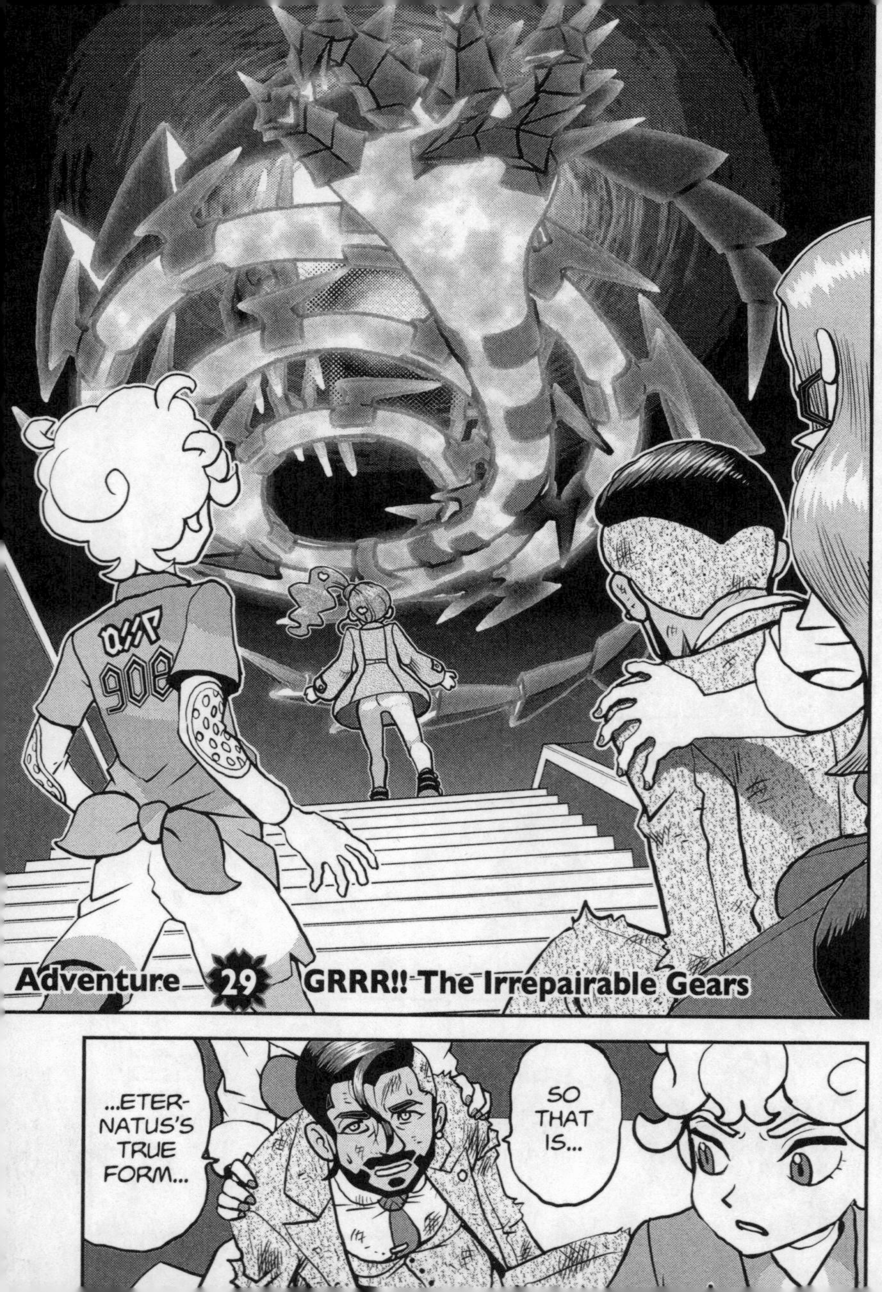
Adventure 29 GRRR!! The Irrepairable Gears
SO THAT IS...
...ETER-NATUS'S TRUE FORM...

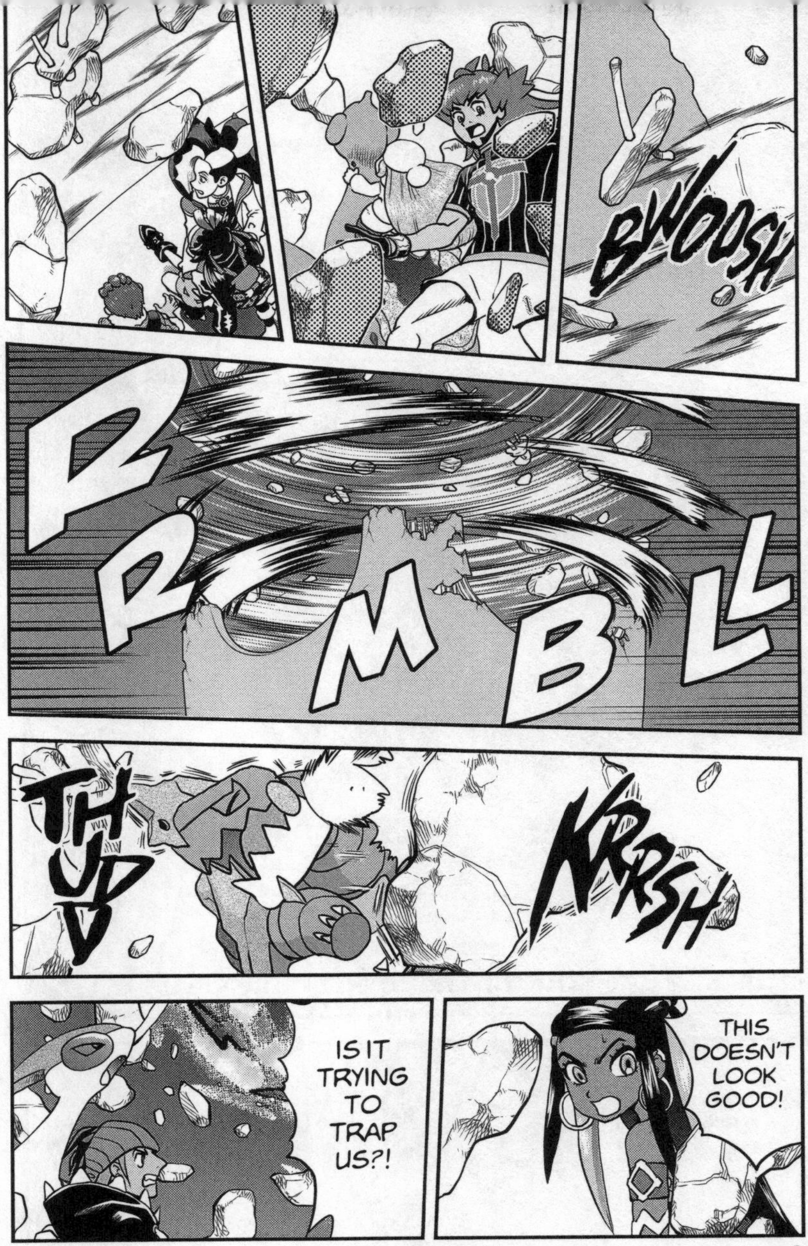
BWOOSH
RRMBLL
KRRSH
THUD
THIS DOESN'T LOOK GOOD!
IS IT TRYING TO TRAP US?!

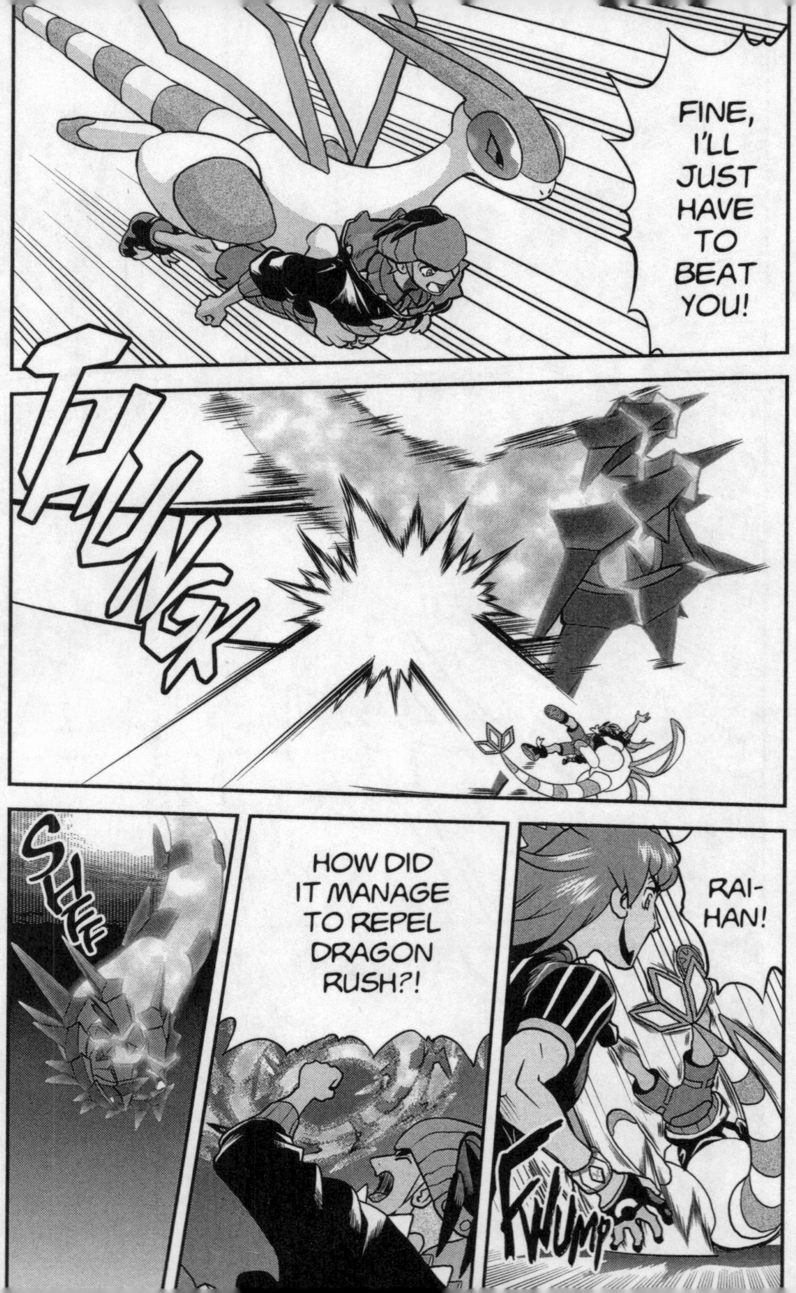
FINE, I'LL JUST HAVE TO BEAT YOU!
THUNGK
RAI-HAN!
FWUMP
HOW DID IT MANAGE TO REPEL DRAGON RUSH?!
SHFF

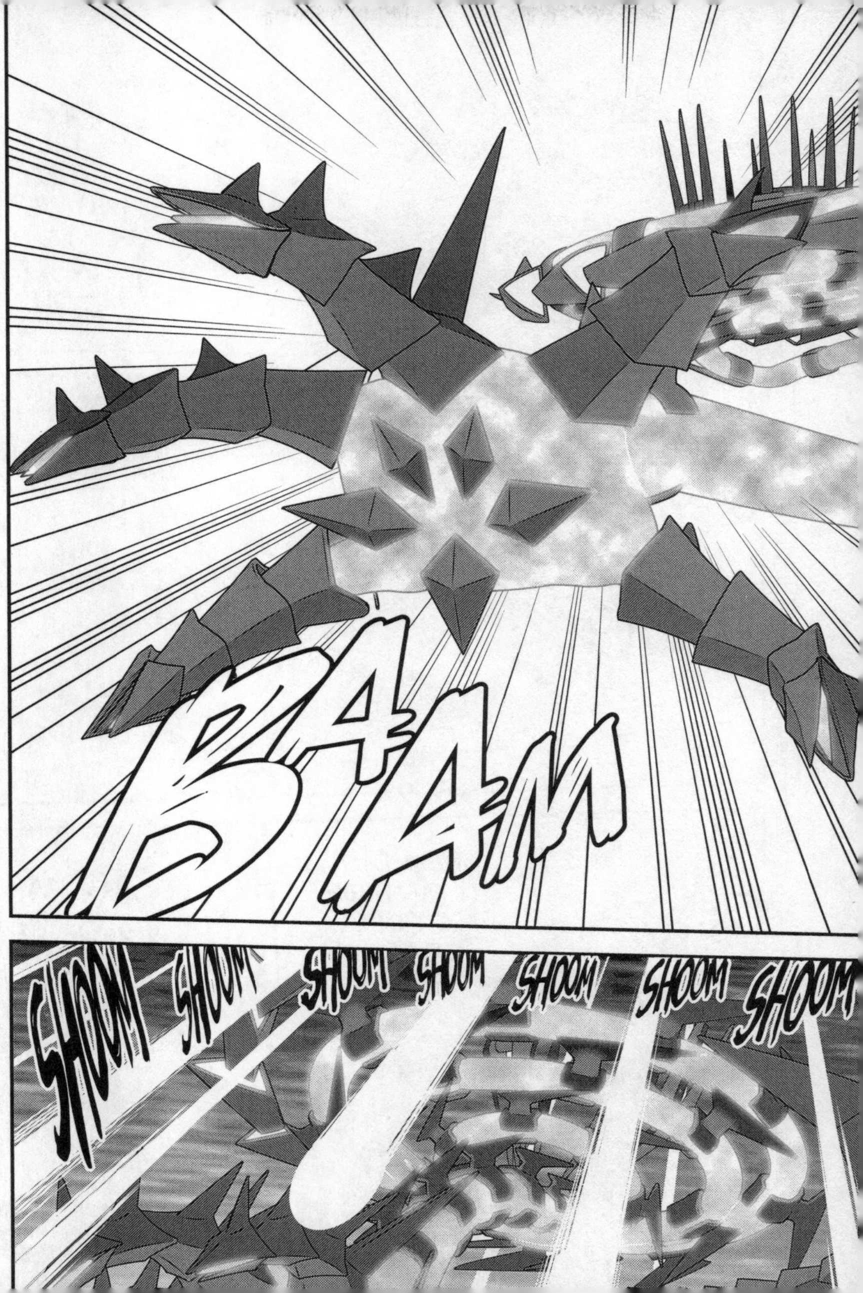
BAM
SHOOM
SHOOM
SHOOM
SHOOM
SHOOM
SHOOM
SHOOM

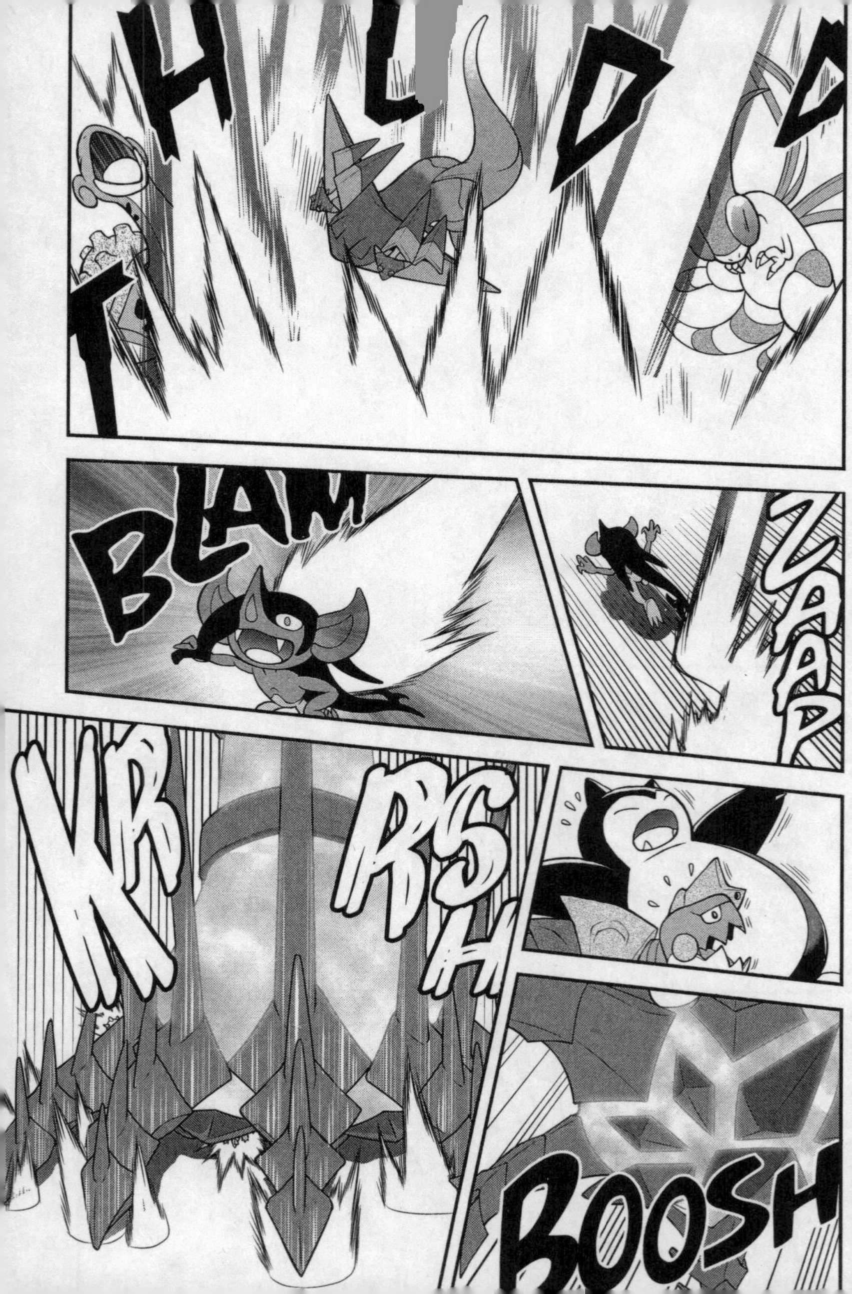
THUDD
ZAAP
BLAM
BOOSH
KRRSH

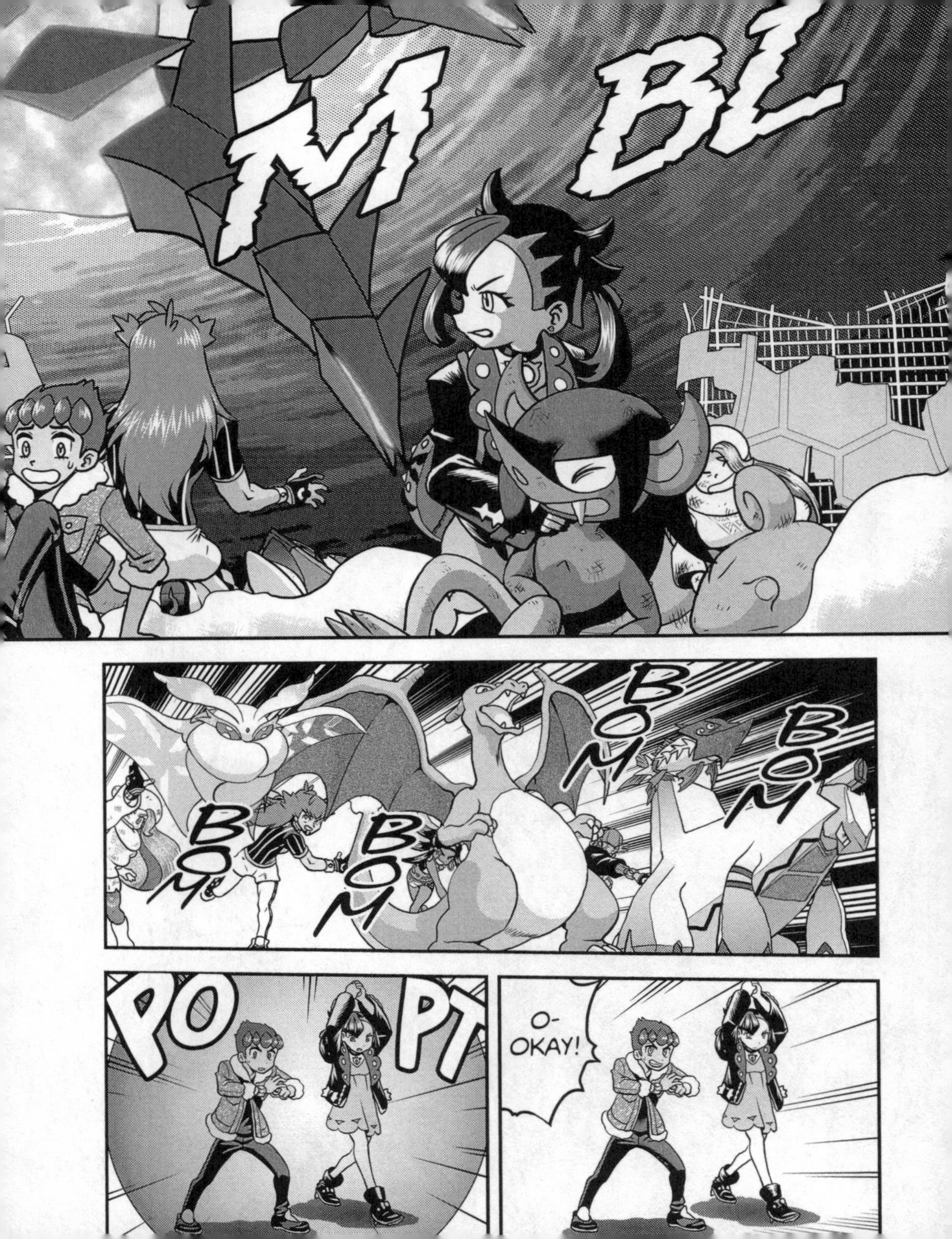
M BL
BOM
BOM
BOM
BOM
O-OKAY!
PO PT

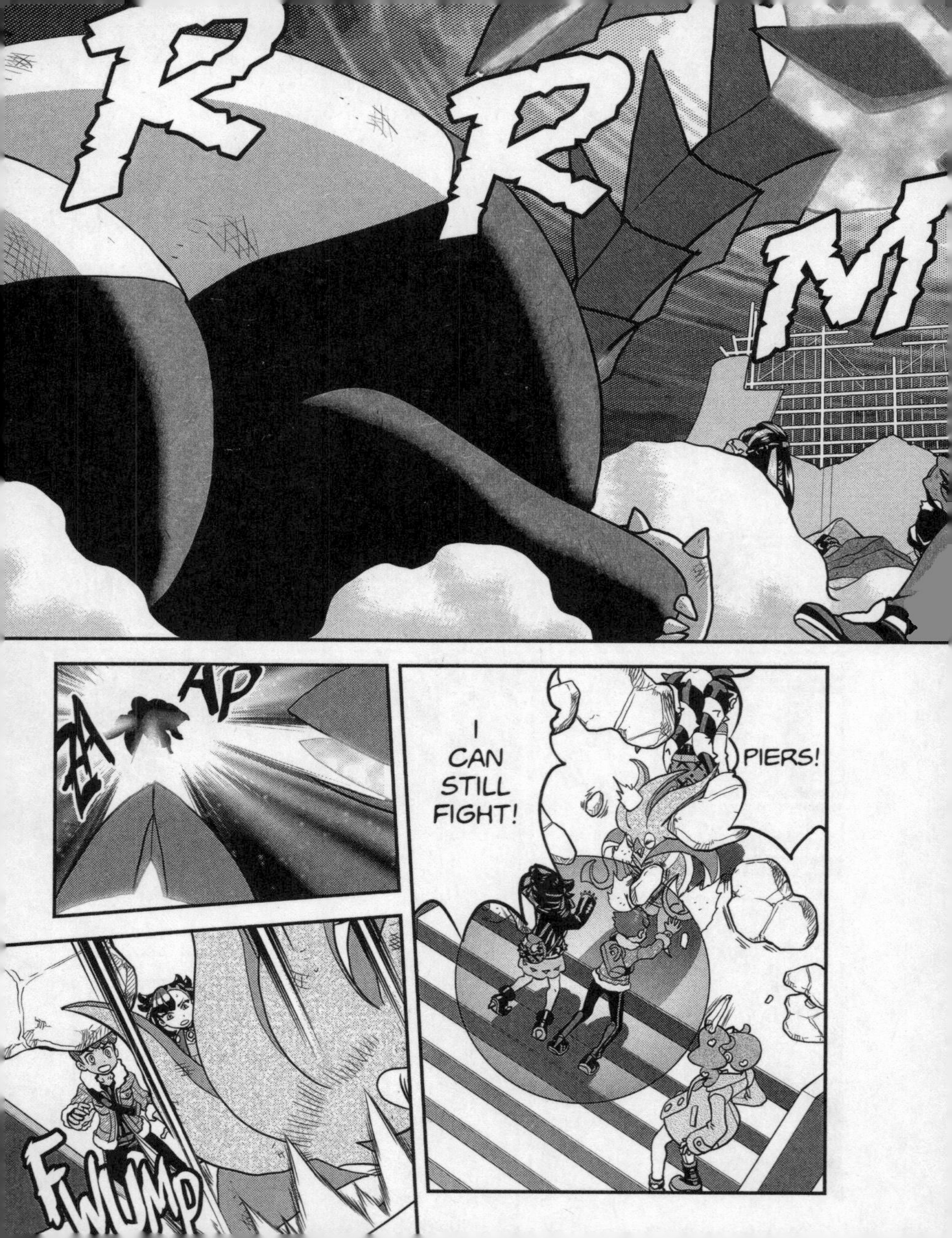
RRM
PIERS!
I CAN STILL FIGHT!
ZAAP
FWUMP

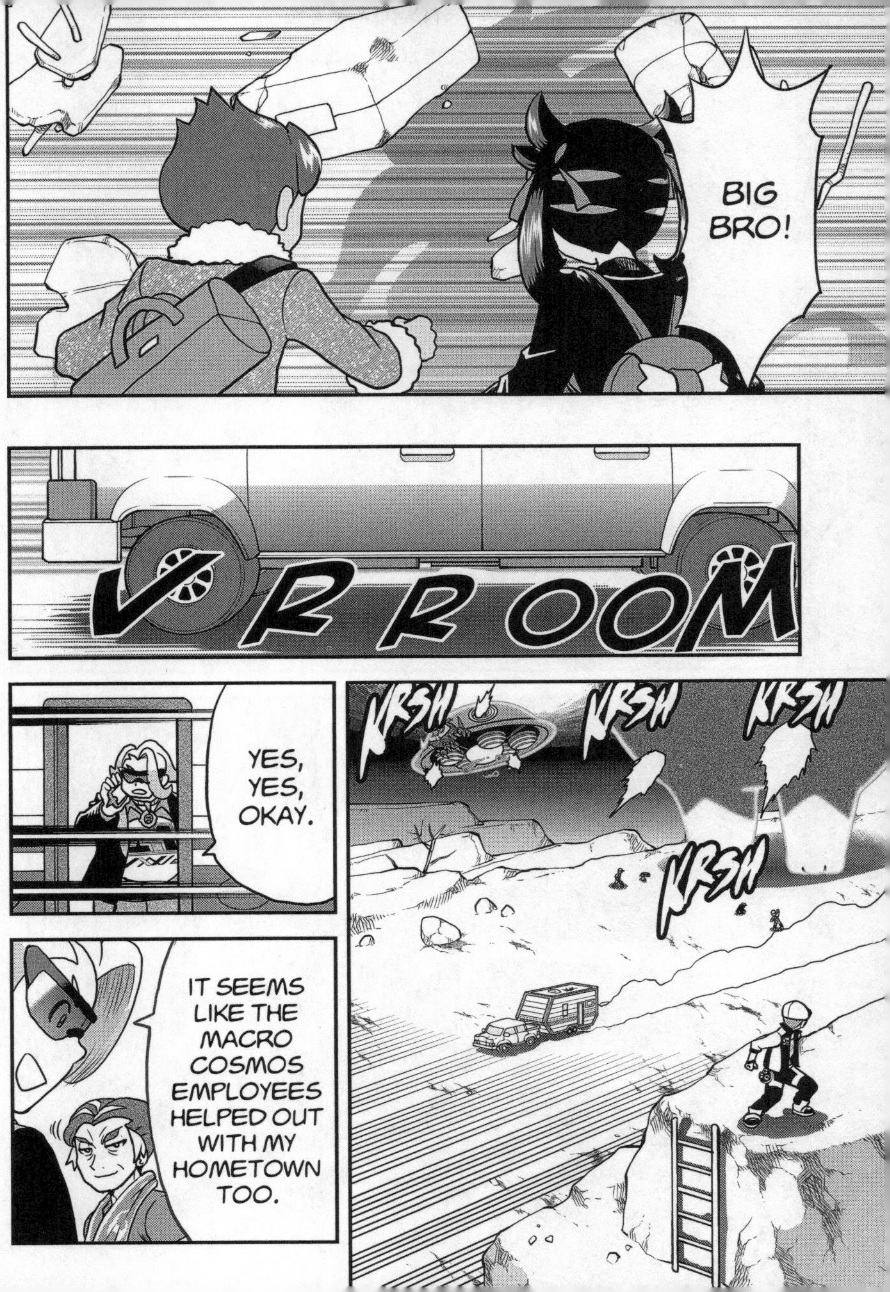
BIG BRO!
VRROOM
KRSH
KRSH
KRSH
KRSH
YES, YES, OKAY.
IT SEEMS LIKE THE MACRO COSMOS EMPLOYEES HELPED OUT WITH MY HOMETOWN TOO.

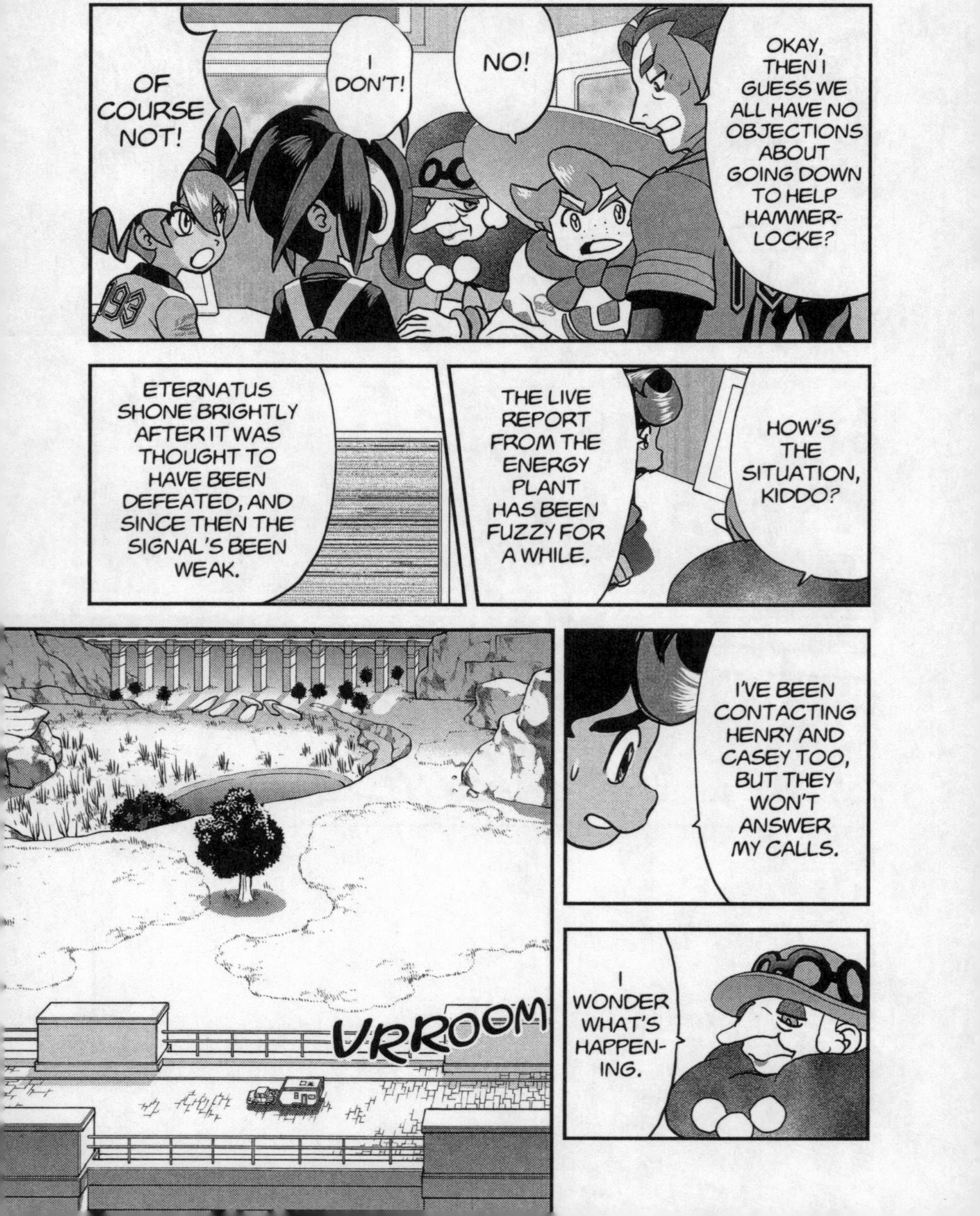
OKAY, THEN I GUESS WE ALL HAVE NO OBJECTIONS ABOUT GOING DOWN TO HELP HAMMER-LOCKE?
NO!
I DON'T!
OF COURSE NOT!
HOW'S THE SITUATION, KIDDO?
THE LIVE REPORT FROM THE ENERGY PLANT HAS BEEN FUZZY FOR A WHILE.
ETERNATUS SHONE BRIGHTLY AFTER IT WAS THOUGHT TO HAVE BEEN DEFEATED, AND SINCE THEN THE SIGNAL'S BEEN WEAK.
I'VE BEEN CONTACTING HENRY AND CASEY TOO, BUT THEY WON'T ANSWER MY CALLS.
I WONDER WHAT'S HAPPEN-ING.
VRROOM

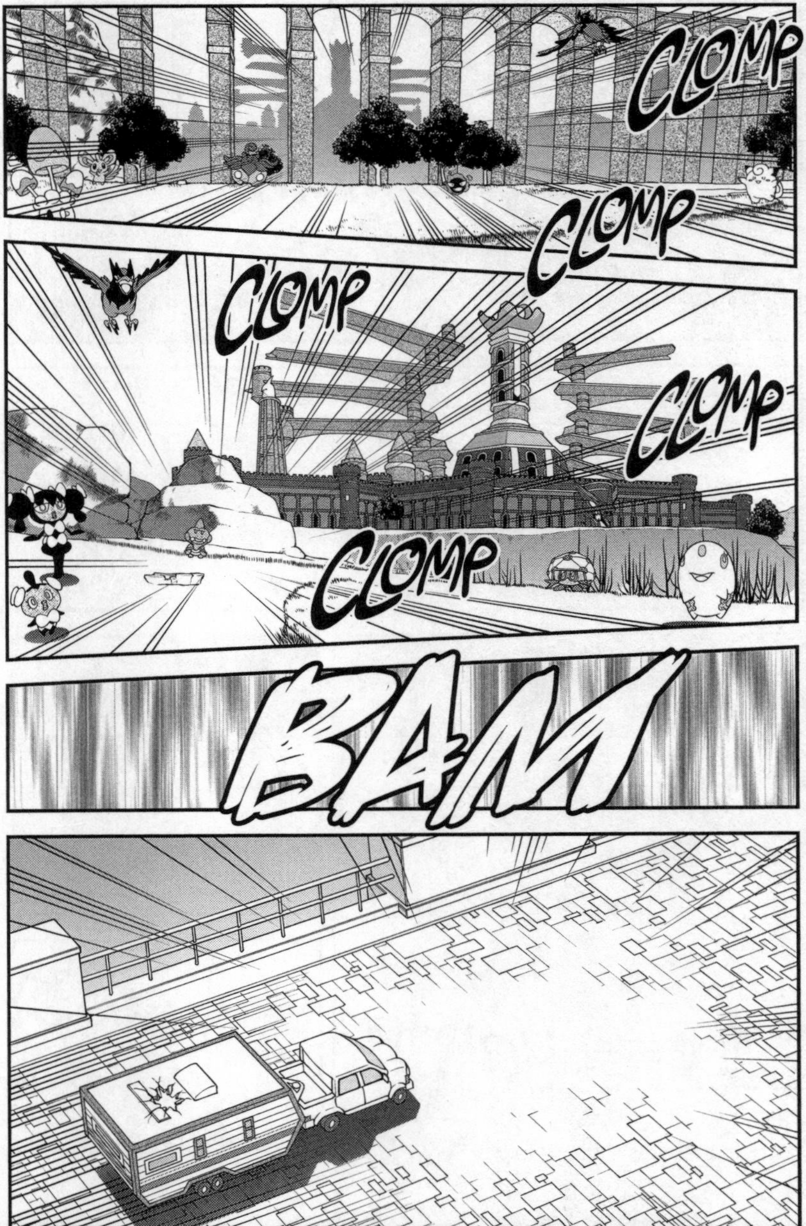
CLOMP
CLOMP
CLOMP
CLOMP
CLOMP
BAM

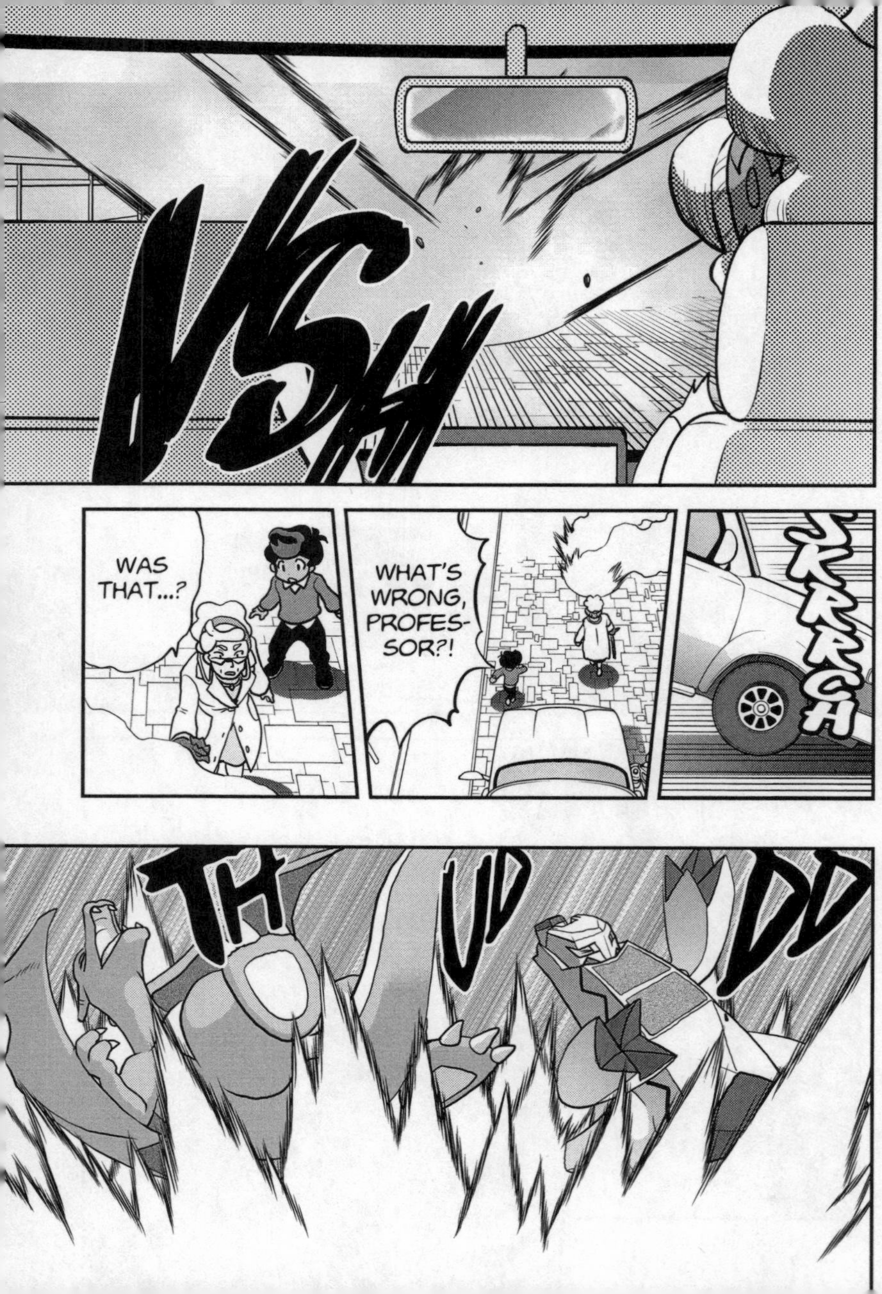
VSHH
SKRRCH
WHAT'S WRONG, PROFESSOR?!
WAS THAT...?
THUDD

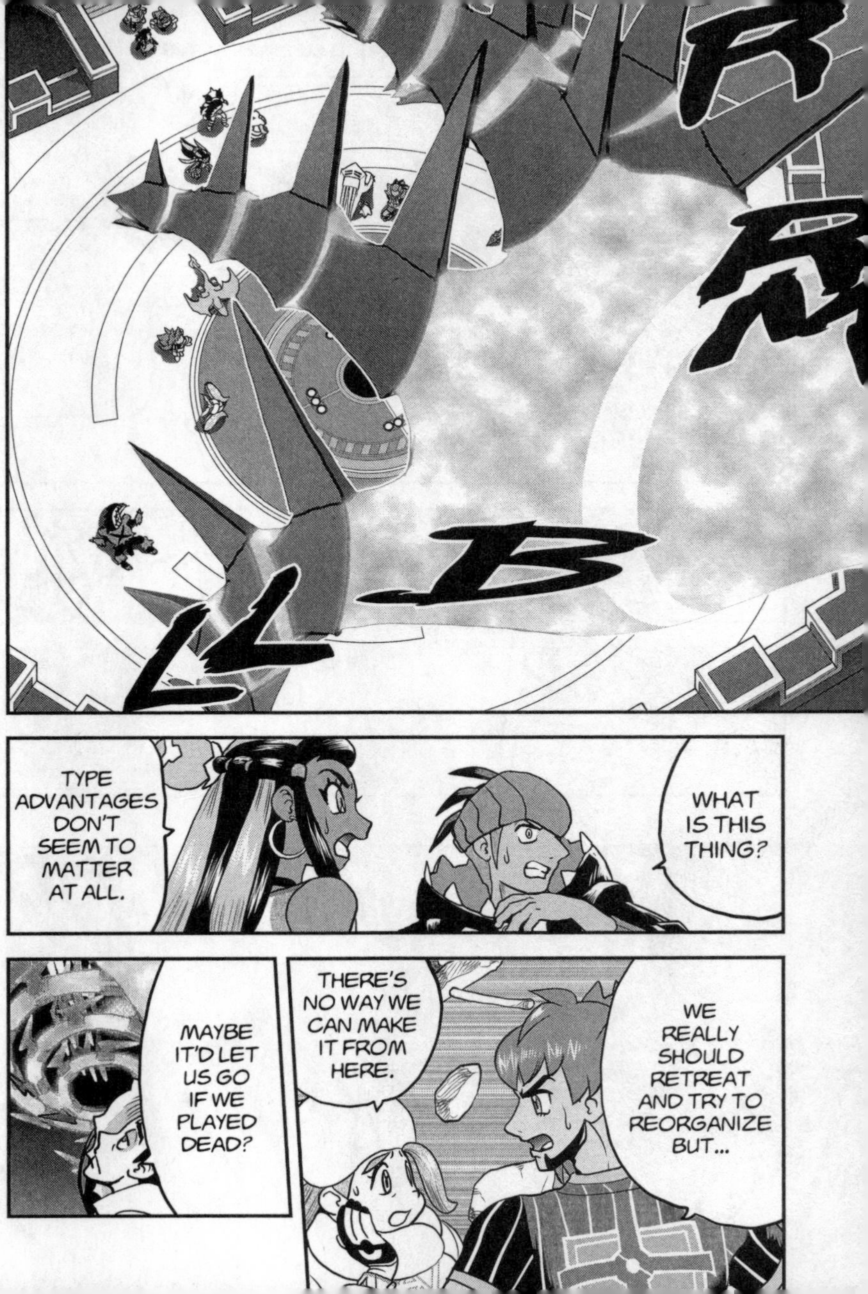
WHAT IS THIS THING?
TYPE ADVANTAGES DON'T SEEM TO MATTER AT ALL.
WE REALLY SHOULD RETREAT AND TRY TO REORGANIZE BUT...
THERE'S NO WAY WE CAN MAKE IT FROM HERE.
MAYBE IT'D LET US GO IF WE PLAYED DEAD?

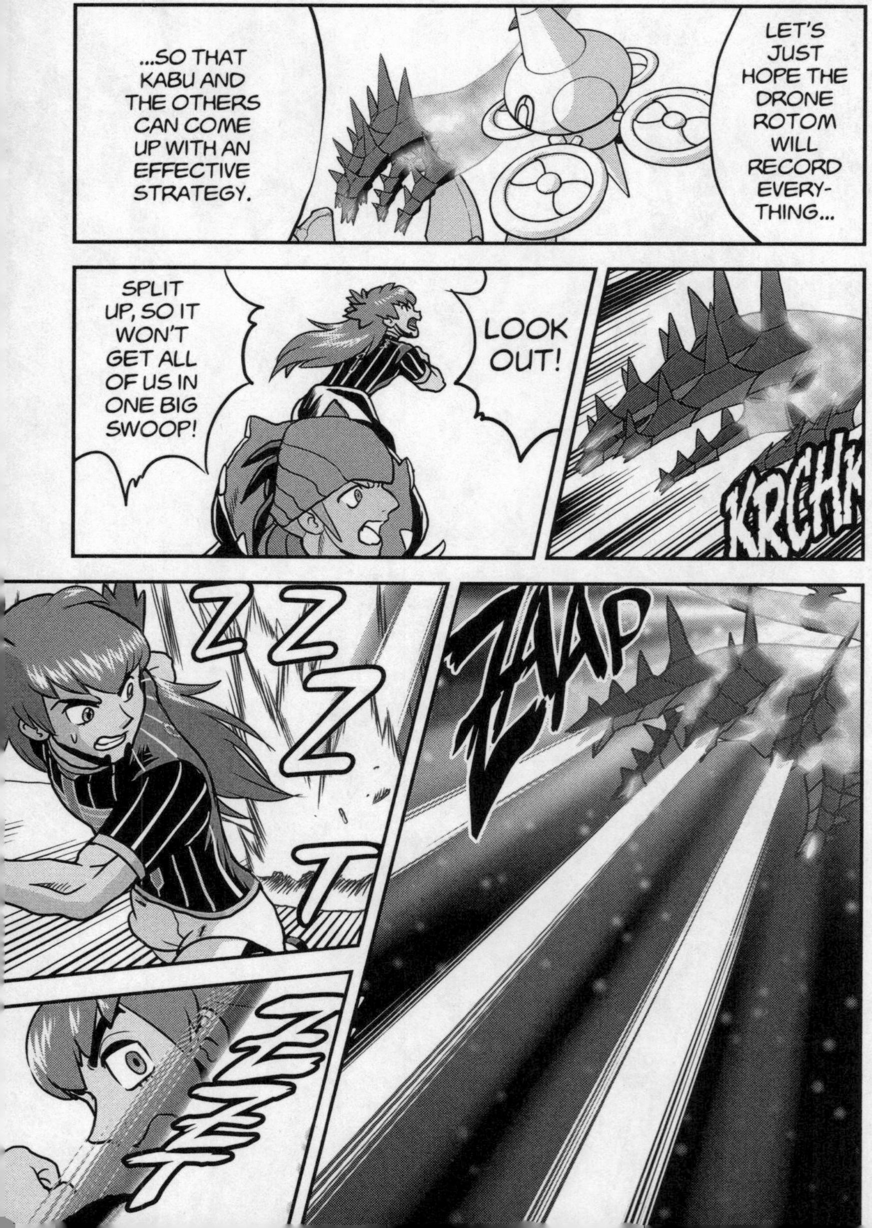
LET'S JUST HOPE THE DRONE ROTOM WILL RECORD EVERY-THING...
...SO THAT KABU AND THE OTHERS CAN COME UP WITH AN EFFECTIVE STRATEGY.
KRCHK
LOOK OUT!
SPLIT UP, SO IT WON'T GET ALL OF US IN ONE BIG SWOOP!
ZAAP
ZZZZT

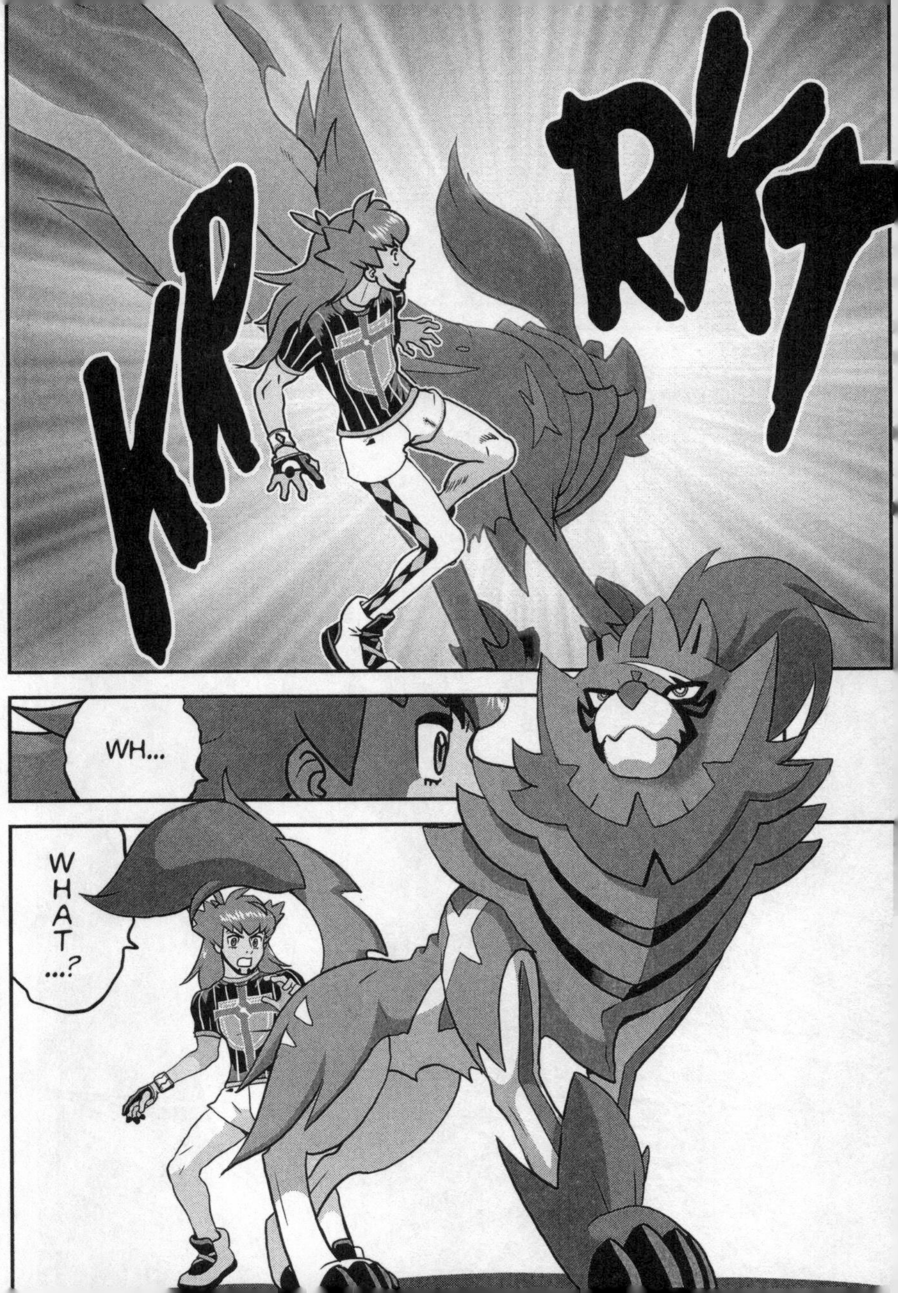
KRRKT
WH...
WHAT...?

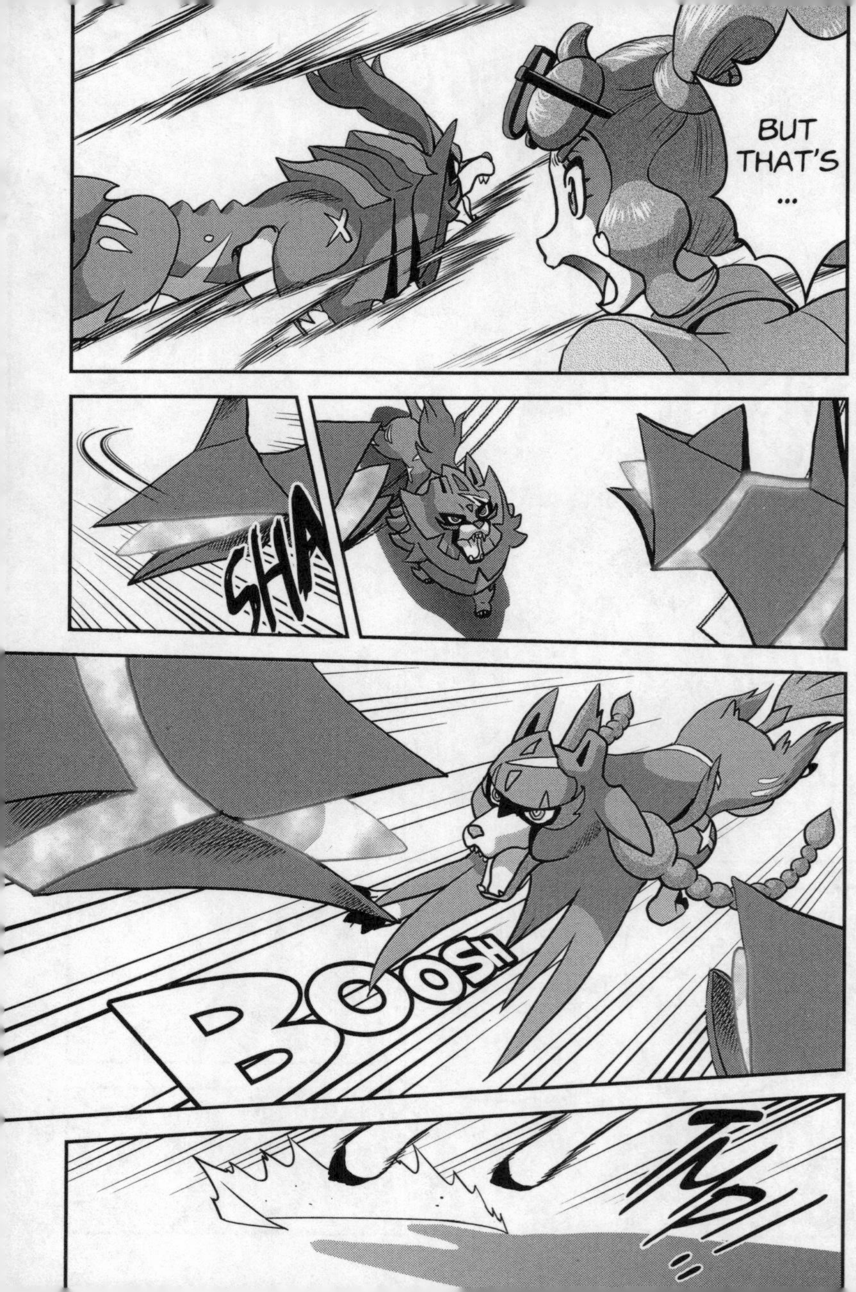
BUT THAT'S ...
SHA
BOOSH
TMP!

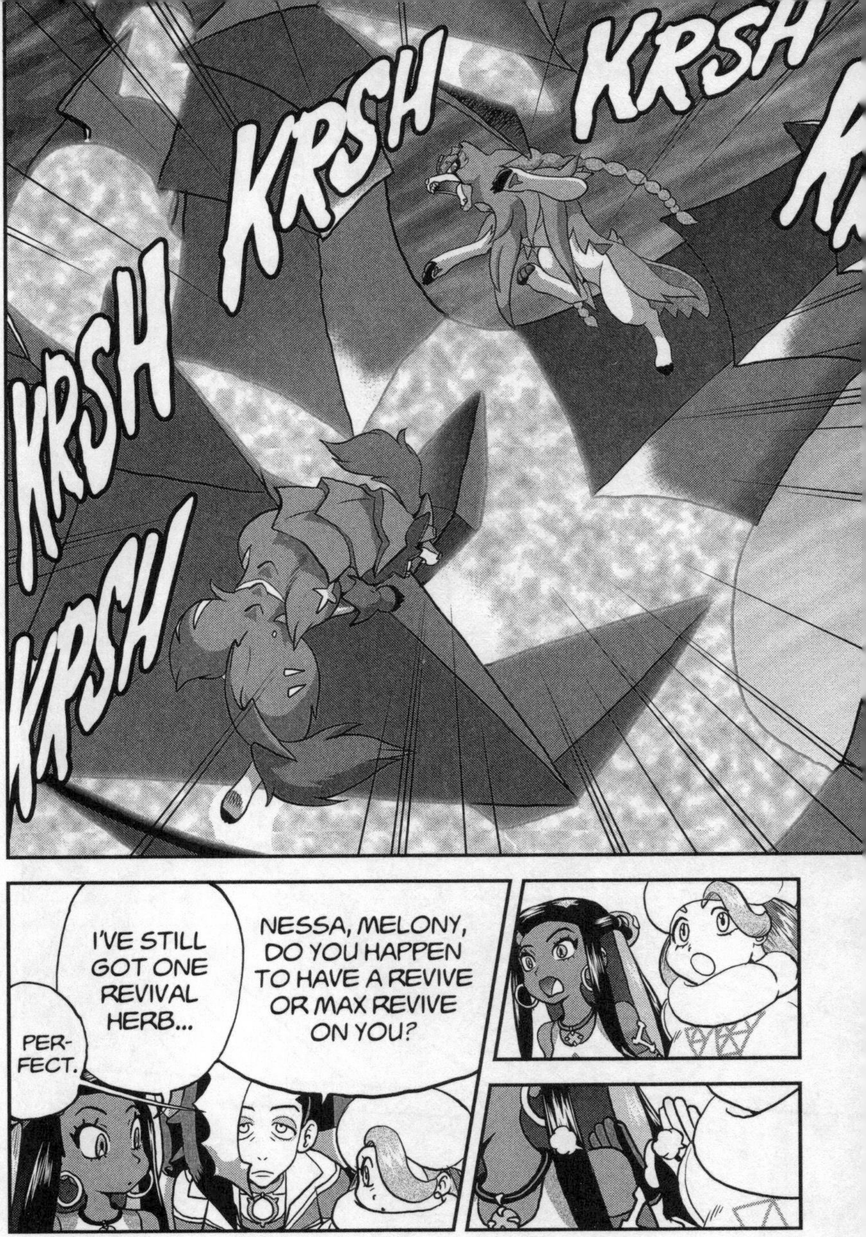
KRSH
KRSH
KRSH
KRSH
NESSA, MELONY, DO YOU HAPPEN TO HAVE A REVIVE OR MAX REVIVE ON YOU?
I'VE STILL GOT ONE REVIVAL HERB...
PER-FECT.

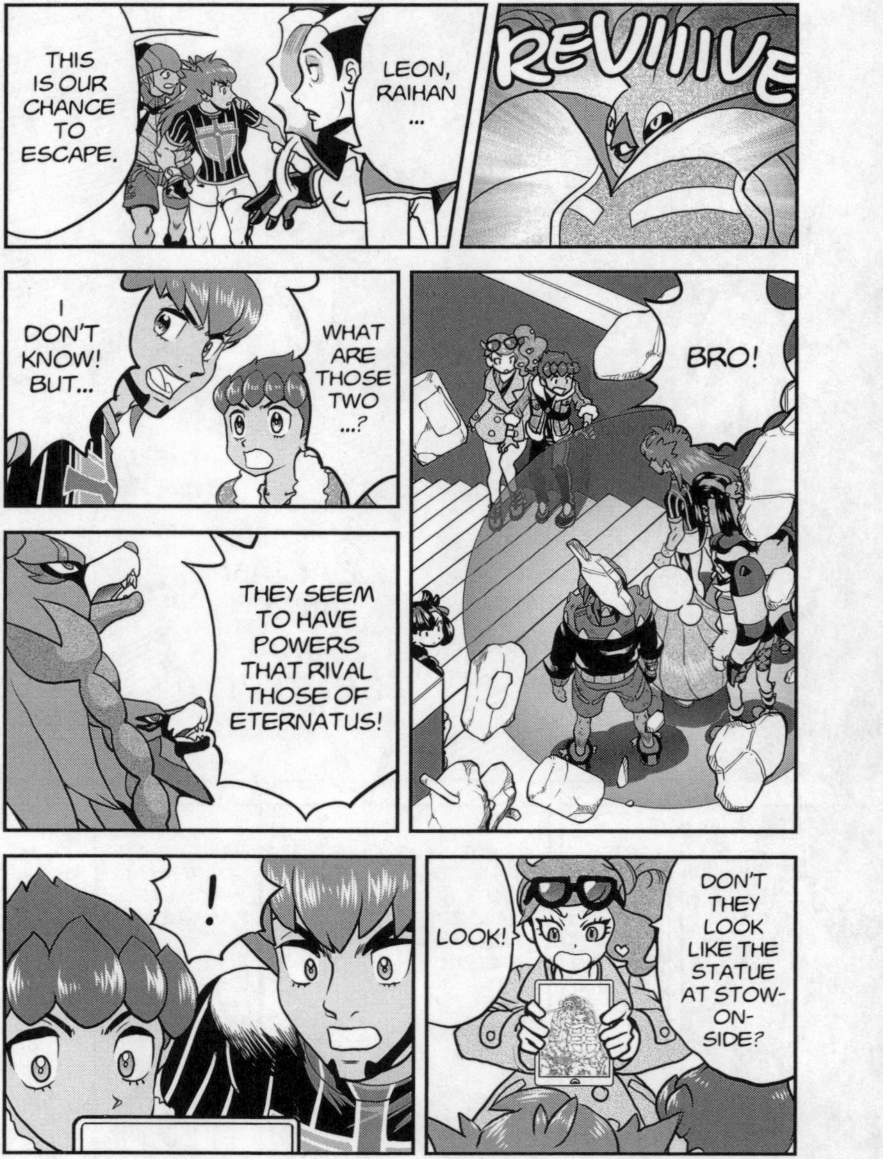
REVIIIVE
LEON, RAIHAN ...
THIS IS OUR CHANCE TO ESCAPE.
BRO!
WHAT ARE THOSE TWO ...?
I DON'T KNOW! BUT...
THEY SEEM TO HAVE POWERS THAT RIVAL THOSE OF ETERNATUS!
DON'T THEY LOOK LIKE THE STATUE AT STOW-ON-SIDE?
LOOK!
!

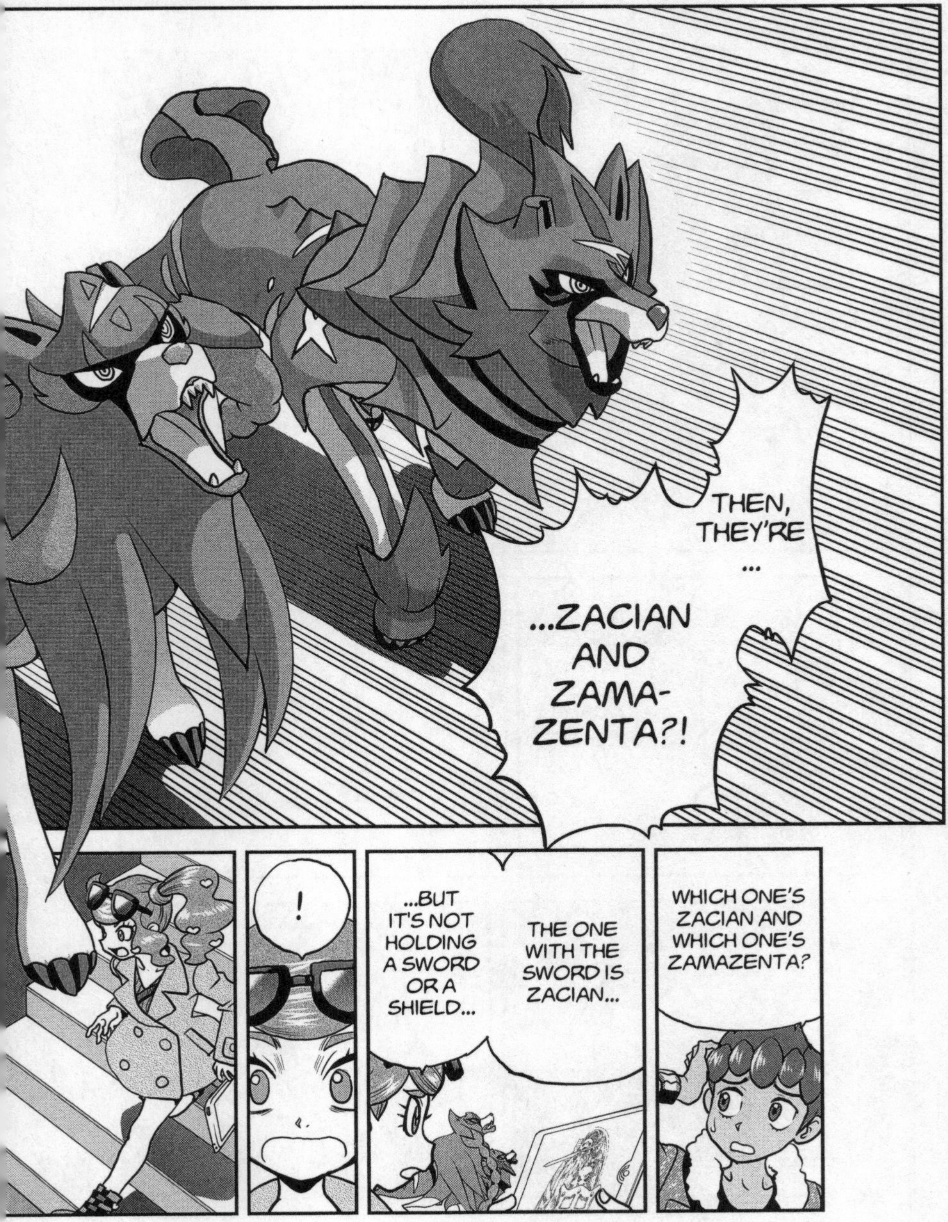
THEN, THEY'RE ...
...ZACIAN AND ZAMA-ZENTA?!
WHICH ONE'S ZACIAN AND WHICH ONE'S ZAMAZENTA?
THE ONE WITH THE SWORD IS ZACIAN...
...BUT IT'S NOT HOLDING A SWORD OR A SHIELD...
!

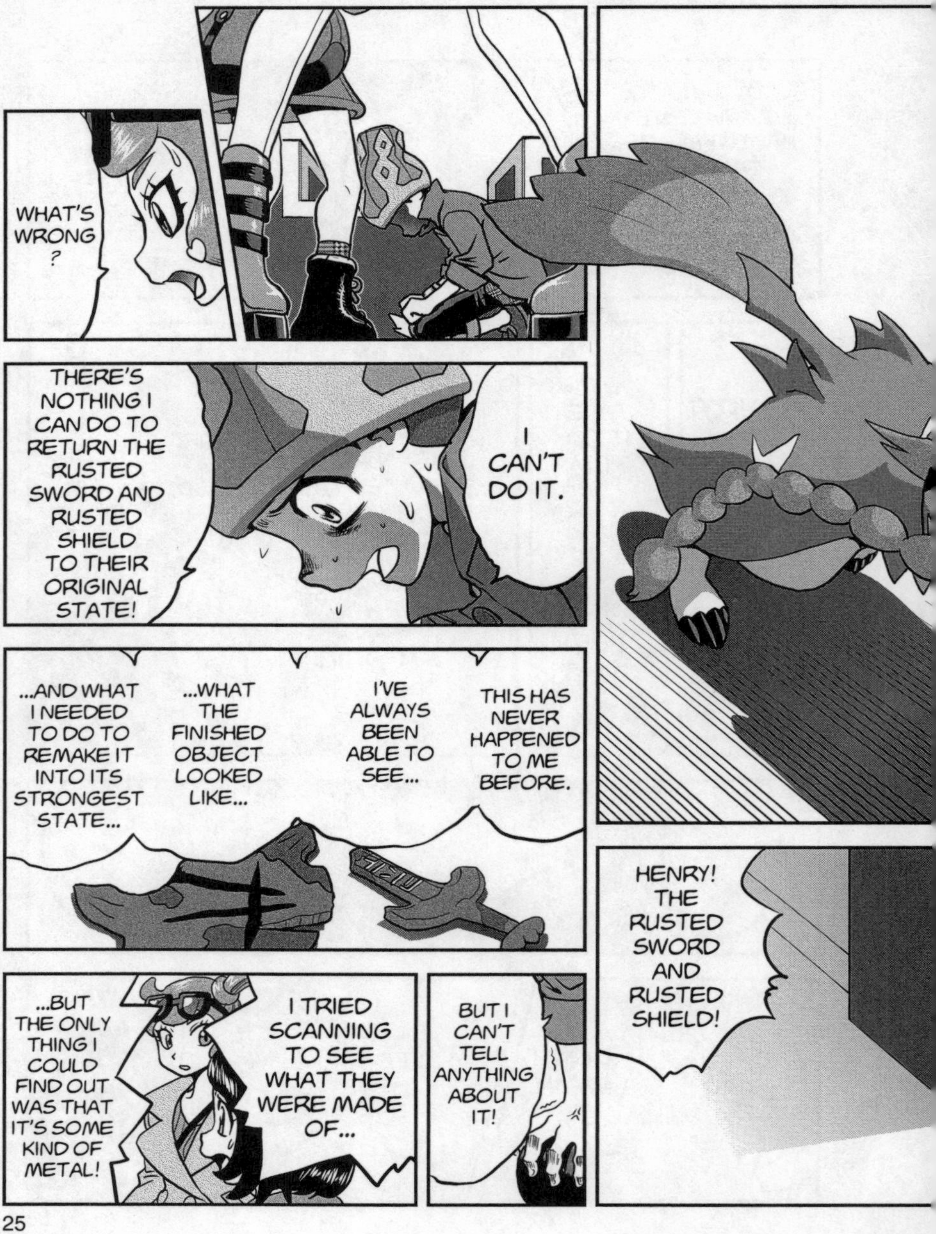
WHAT'S WRONG?
I CAN'T DO IT.
THERE'S NOTHING I CAN DO TO RETURN THE RUSTED SWORD AND RUSTED SHIELD TO THEIR ORIGINAL STATE!
THIS HAS NEVER HAPPENED TO ME BEFORE.
I'VE ALWAYS BEEN ABLE TO SEE...
...WHAT THE FINISHED OBJECT LOOKED LIKE...
...AND WHAT I NEEDED TO DO TO REMAKE IT INTO ITS STRONGEST STATE...
HENRY! THE RUSTED SWORD AND RUSTED SHIELD!
BUT I CAN'T TELL ANYTHING ABOUT IT!
I TRIED SCANNING TO SEE WHAT THEY WERE MADE OF...
...BUT THE ONLY THING I COULD FIND OUT WAS THAT IT'S SOME KIND OF METAL!

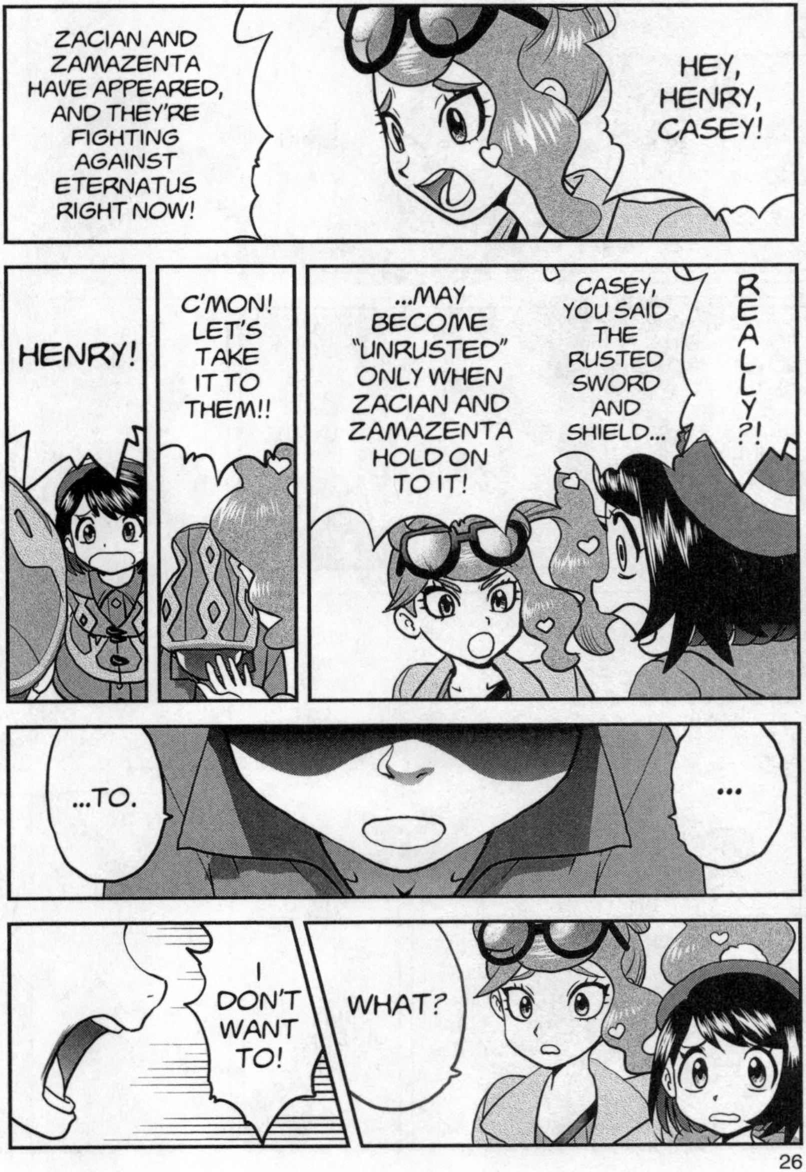
HEY, HENRY, CASEY!
ZACIAN AND ZAMAZENTA HAVE APPEARED, AND THEY'RE FIGHTING AGAINST ETERNATUS RIGHT NOW!
REALLY?!
CASEY, YOU SAID THE RUSTED SWORD AND SHIELD...
...MAY BECOME "UNRUSTED" ONLY WHEN ZACIAN AND ZAMAZENTA HOLD ON TO IT!
C'MON! LET'S TAKE IT TO THEM!!
HENRY!
...
...TO.
WHAT?
I DON'T WANT TO!

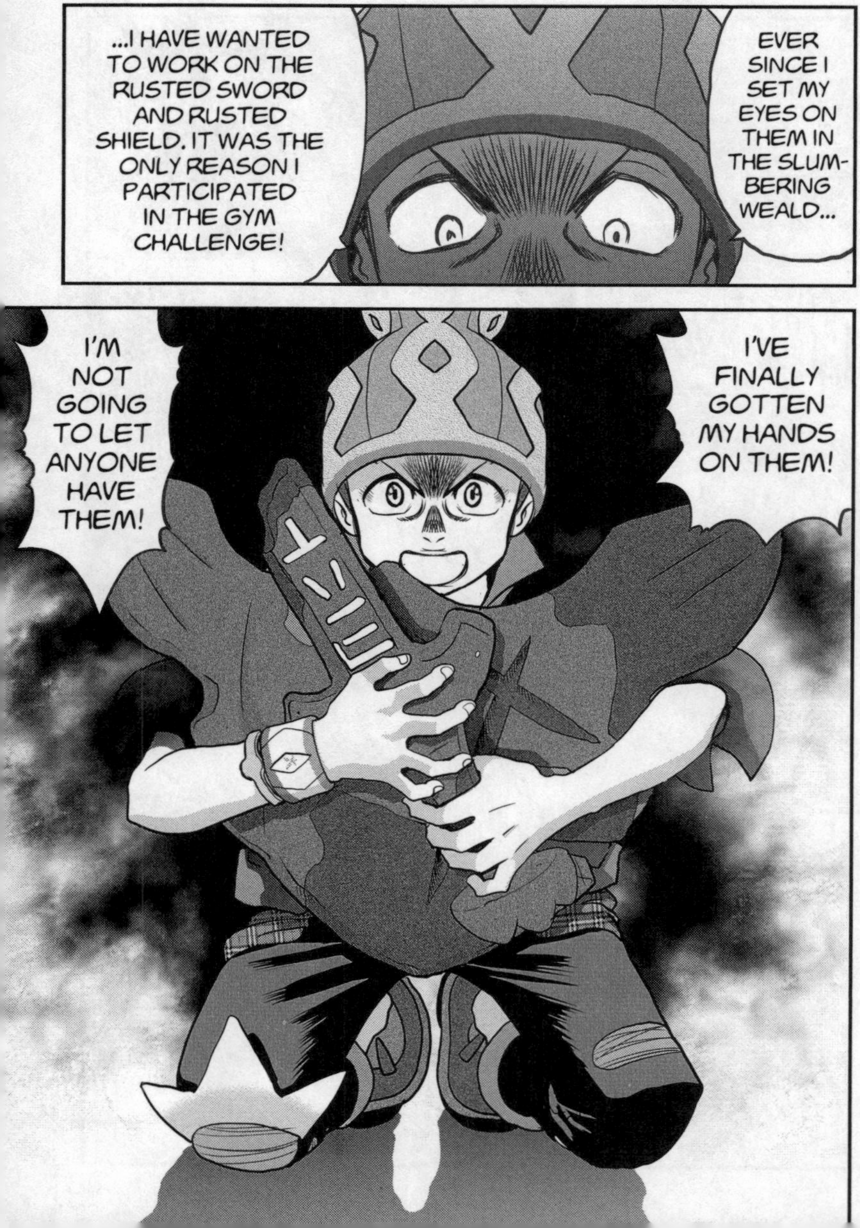
EVER SINCE I SET MY EYES ON THEM IN THE SLUMBERING WEALD...
...I HAVE WANTED TO WORK ON THE RUSTED SWORD AND RUSTED SHIELD. IT WAS THE ONLY REASON I PARTICIPATED IN THE GYM CHALLENGE!
I'VE FINALLY GOTTEN MY HANDS ON THEM!
I'M NOT GOING TO LET ANYONE HAVE THEM!

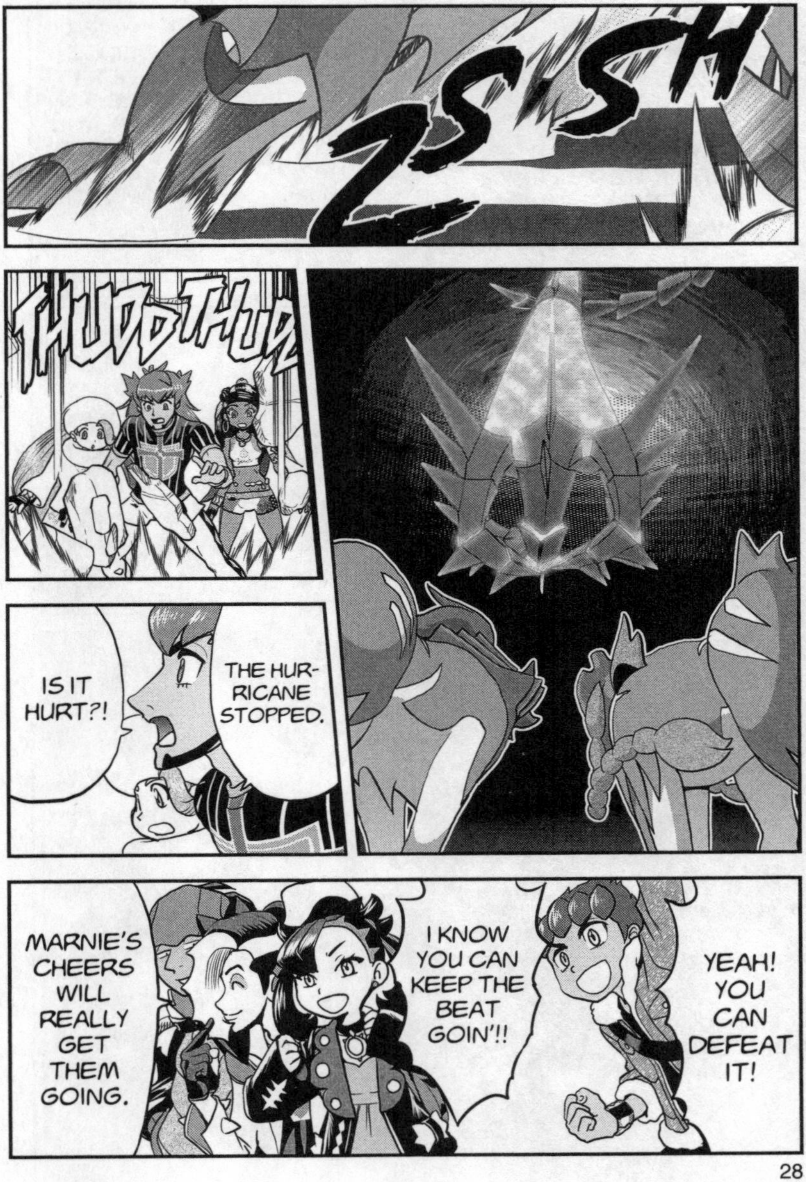

ZSSH
THUD THUD
THE HURRICANE STOPPED.
IS IT HURT?!
YEAH! YOU CAN DEFEAT IT!
I KNOW YOU CAN KEEP THE BEAT GOIN'!!
MARNIE'S CHEERS WILL REALLY GET THEM GOING.

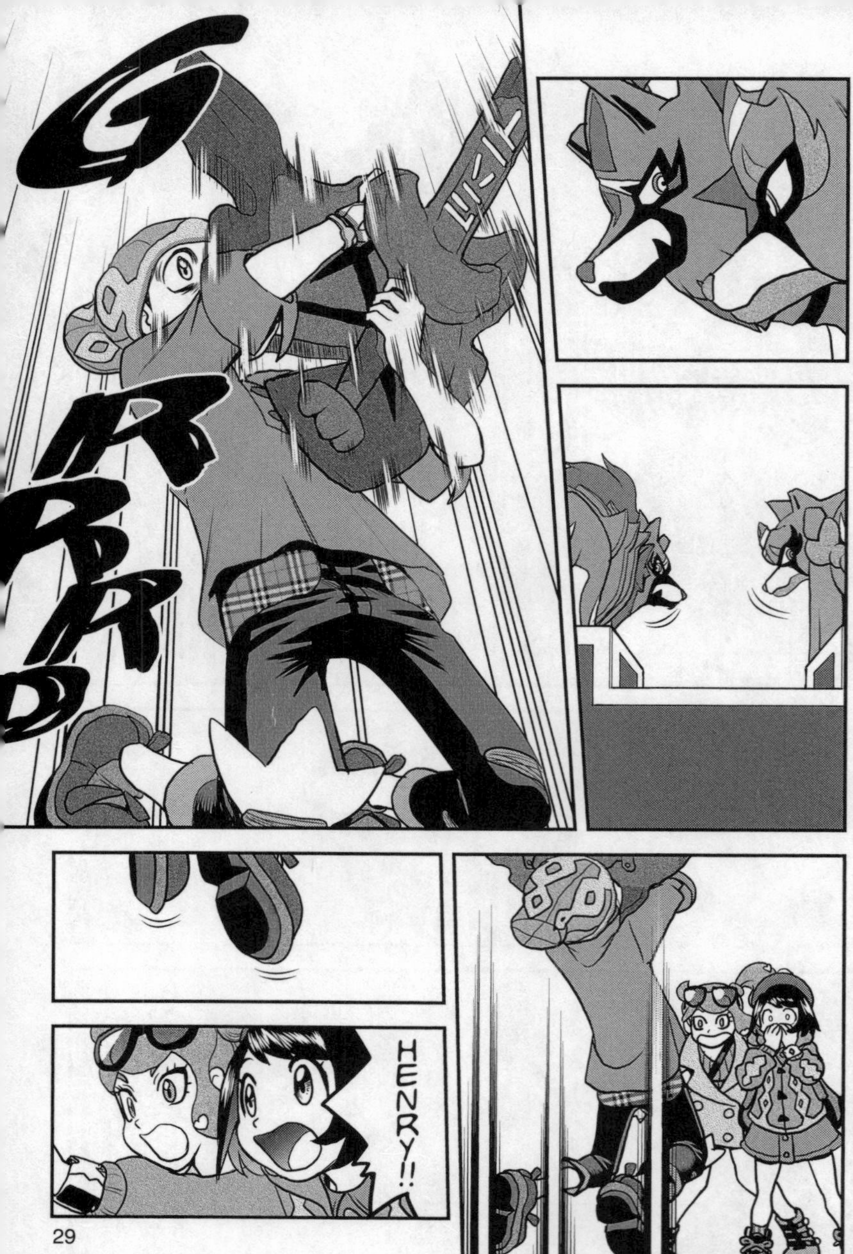
GRRRD
HENRY!!

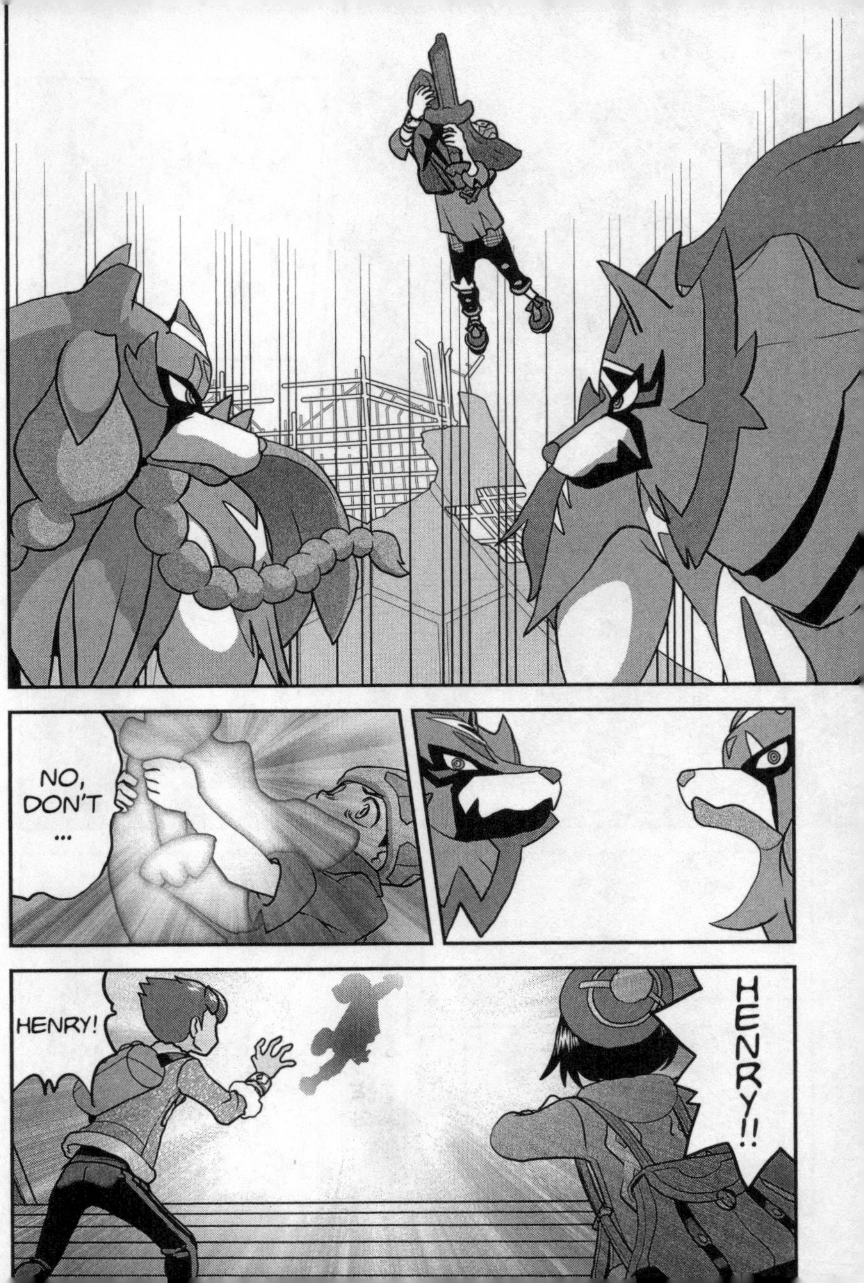
NO, DON'T ...
HENRY!!
HENRY!

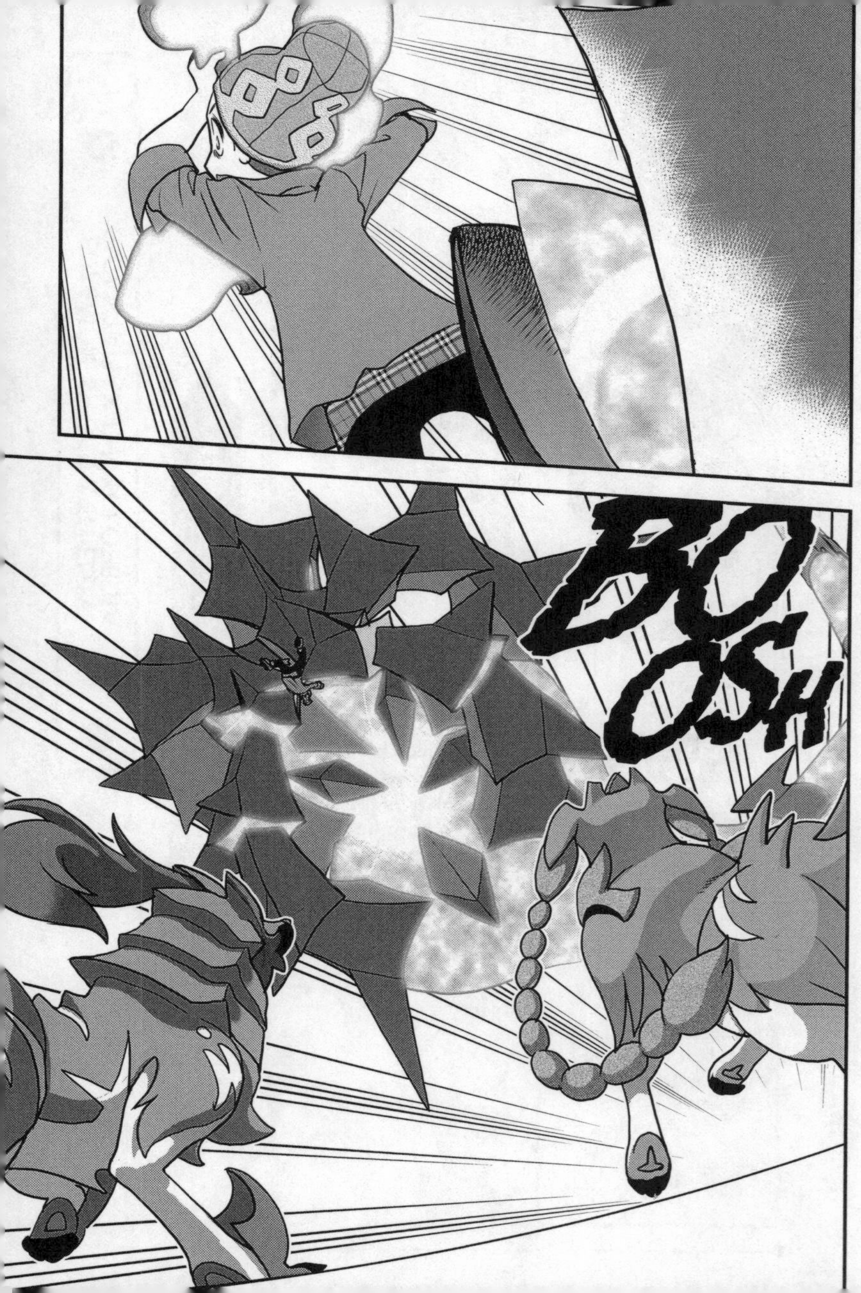
BOOOSH

GIGANTAMAX CHARIZARD

HEIGHT	91'10"+
WEIGHT	??? lbs

ORDINARY
CHARIZARD

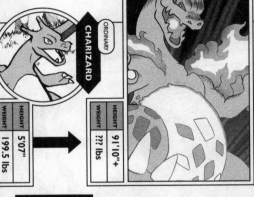

HEIGHT	5'07"
WEIGHT	199.5 lbs

TYPE	Fire, Flying
ABILITY	Blaze
G-MAX MOVE	G-Max Wildfire

Gigantamax Charizard has flaming wings, and a huge pillar of fire rises from the horn on its head. Also, diamond-shaped markings adorn its stomach and knees. The flame inside its body is as hot as magma, and the more Charizard roars, the hotter it gets!!

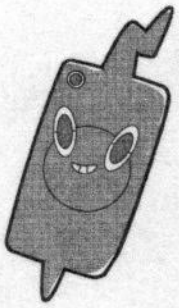

STRATEGY NOTES

The Fire-type move used by a Gigantamax Charizard is G-Max Wildfire. This powerful move is very dangerous. The fiery flames are said to be more than 3,600 degrees Fahrenheit. Whether you can bear that heat will decide if you will win or lose the battle!

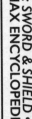

Adventure 30 Oh My!! The Disappearance of Henry

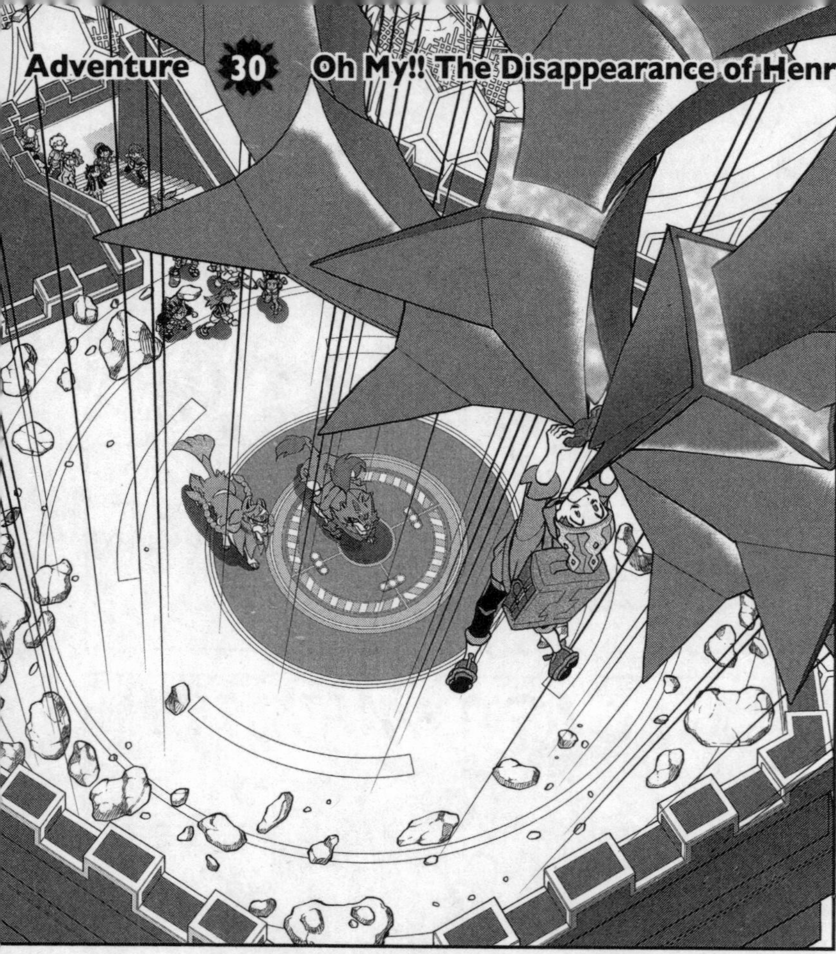

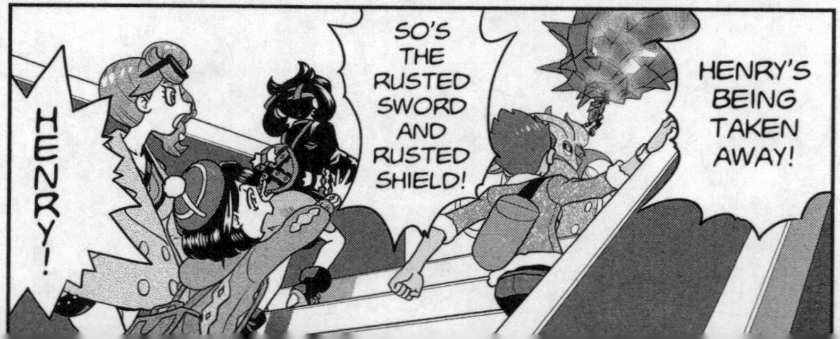
HENRY'S BEING TAKEN AWAY!
SO'S THE RUSTED SWORD AND RUSTED SHIELD!
HENRY!

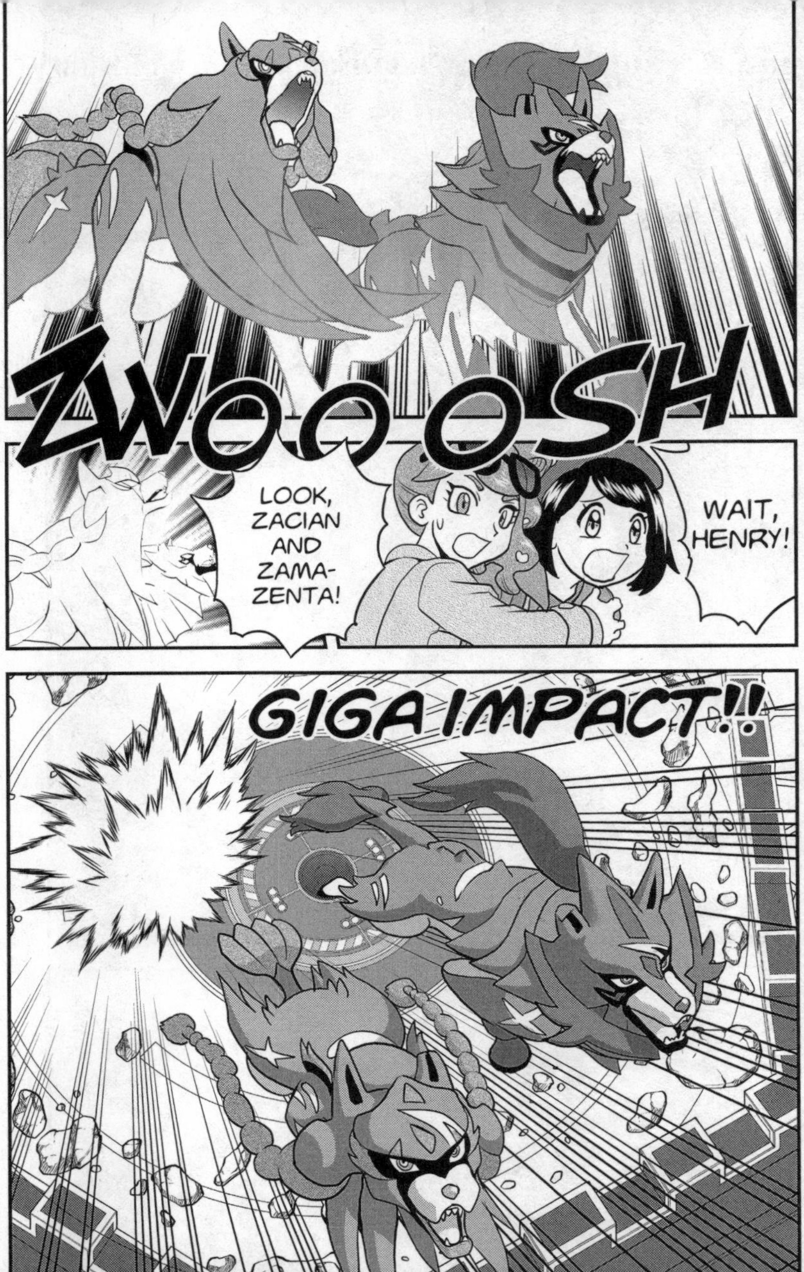
ZWOOOSH
WAIT, HENRY!
LOOK, ZACIAN AND ZAMA-ZENTA!
GIGA IMPACT!!

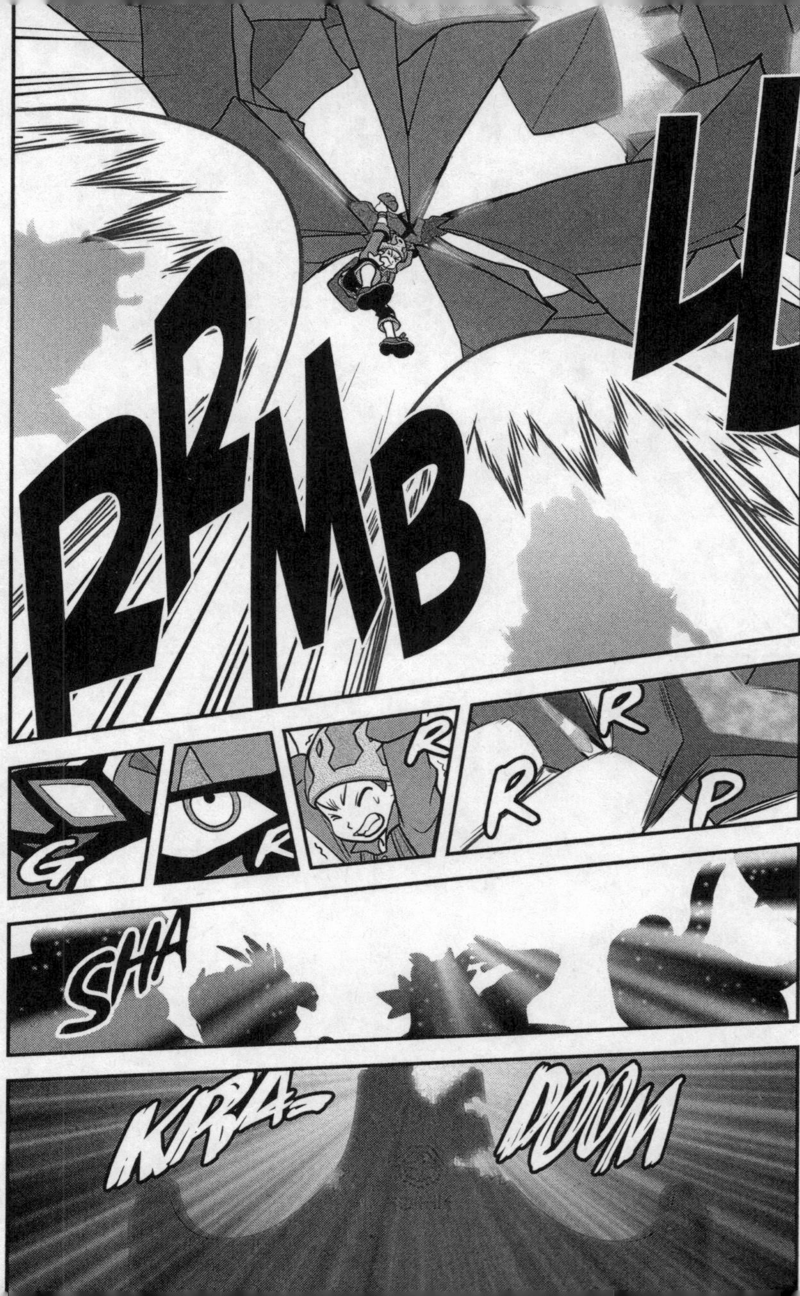
RRMBLL
R
R
R
P
R
K
G
SHA
KRA–
DOOM

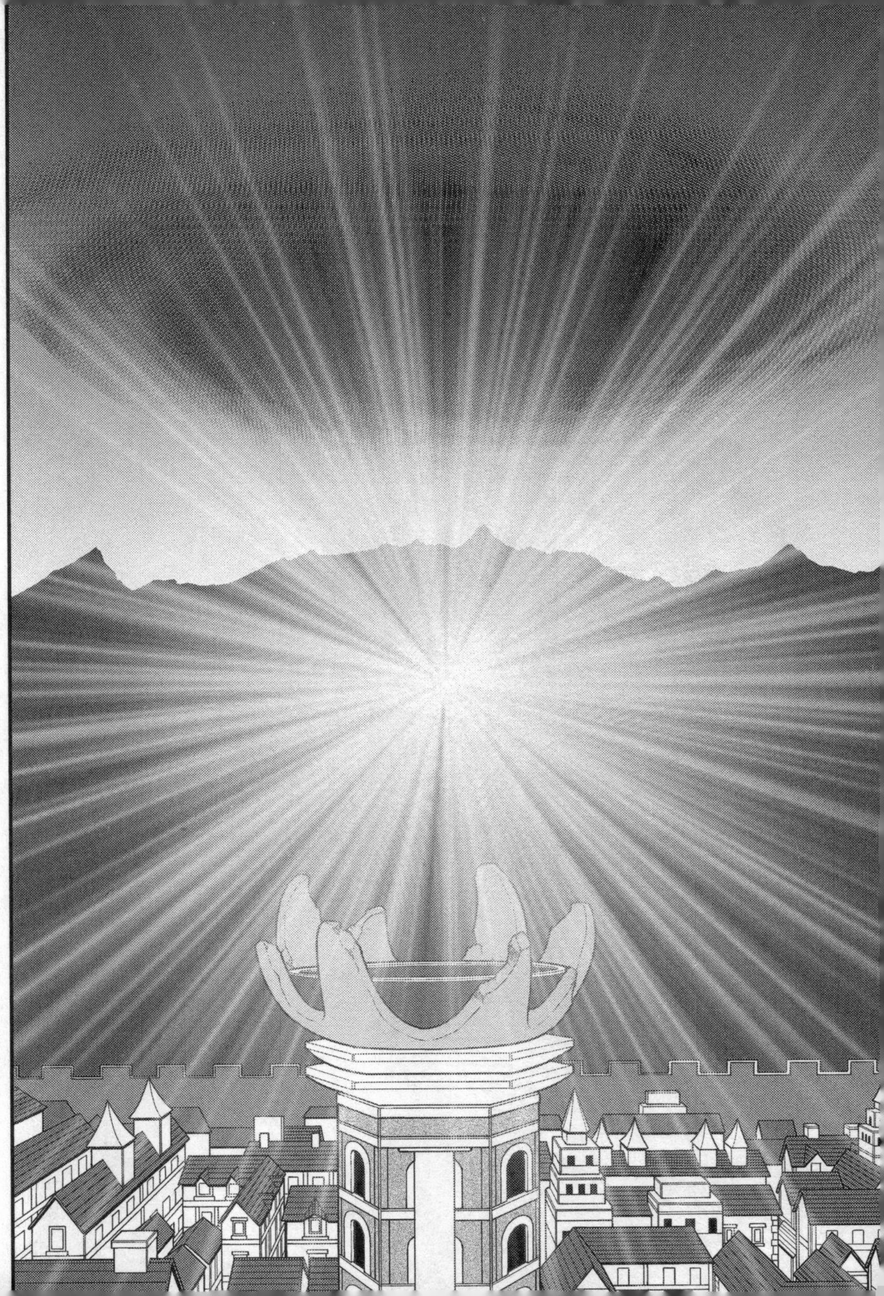

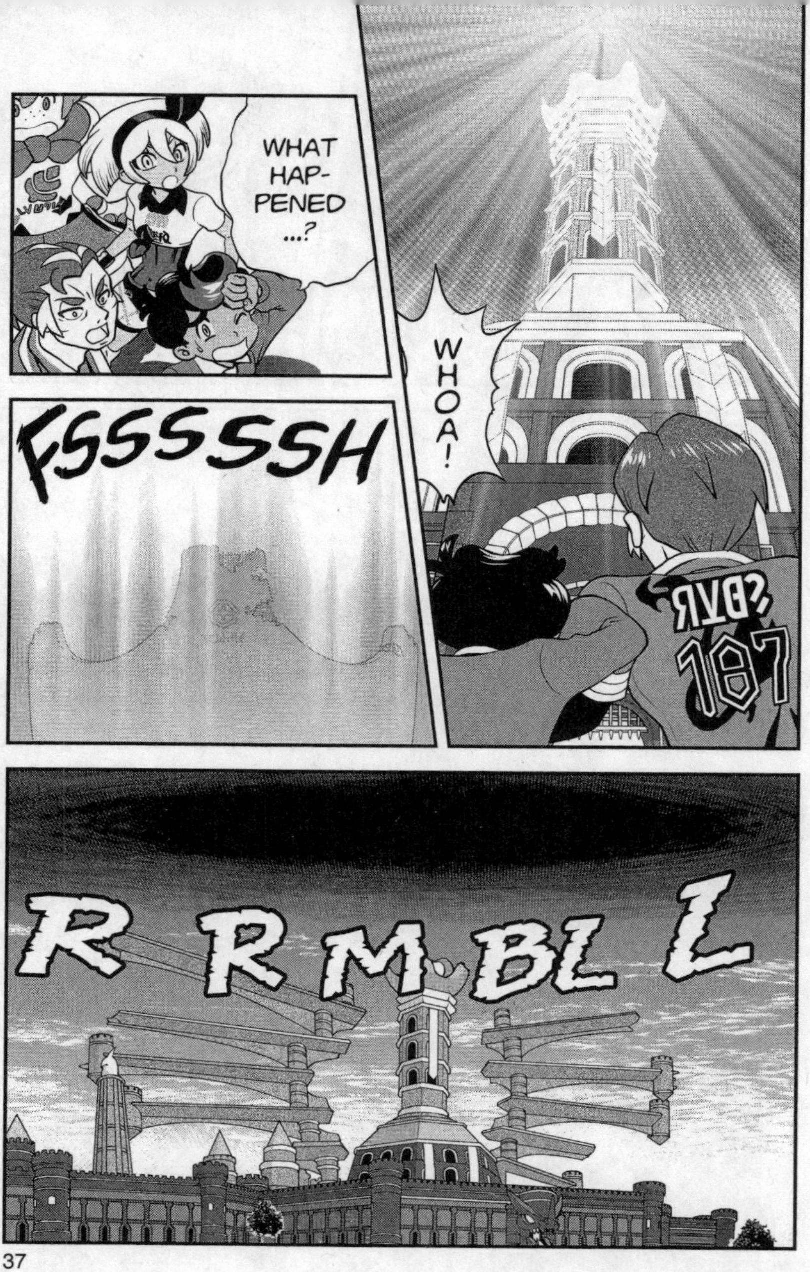
WHOA!
WHAT HAP-PENED ...?
FSSSSSH
R R M BL L

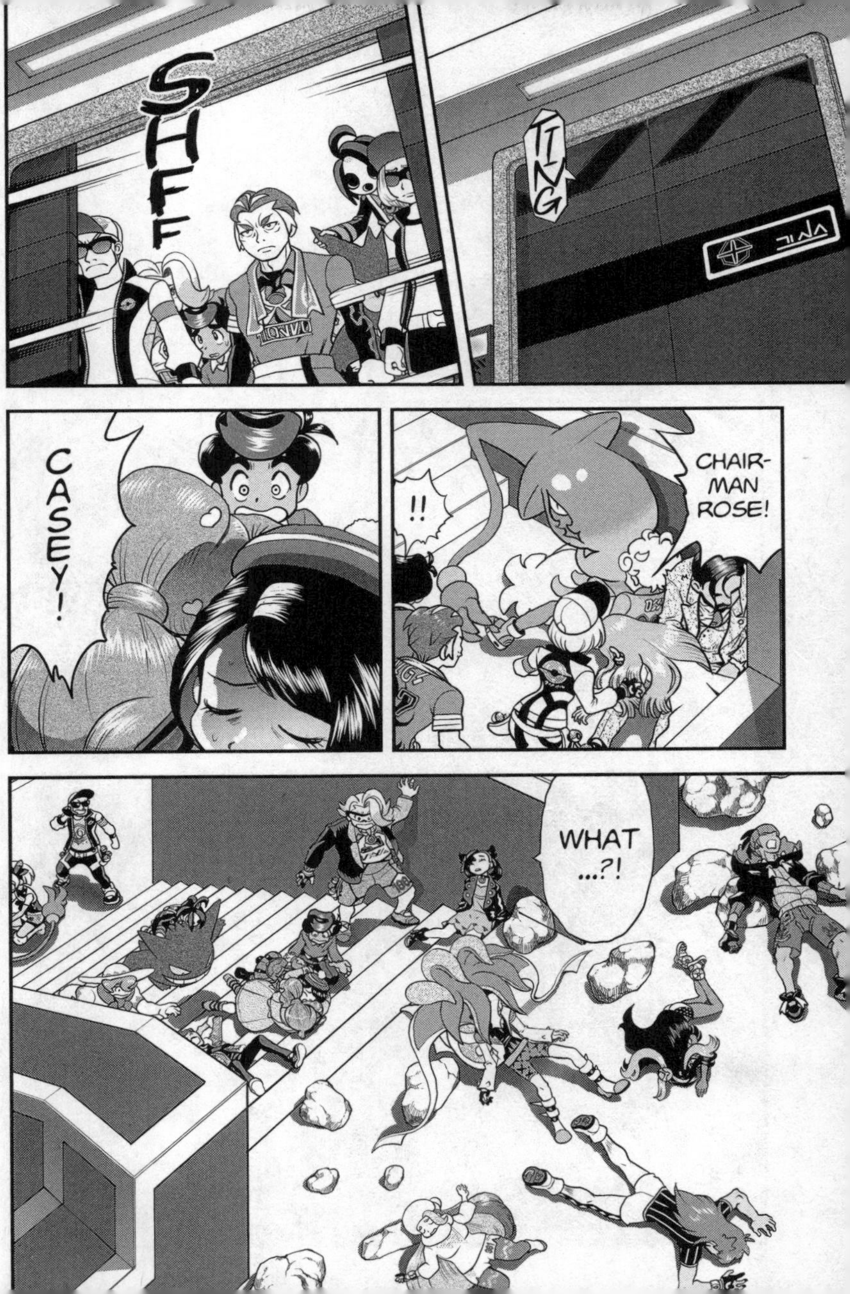
TING
SHFF
CHAIR-MAN ROSE!
!!
CASEY!
WHAT ...?!

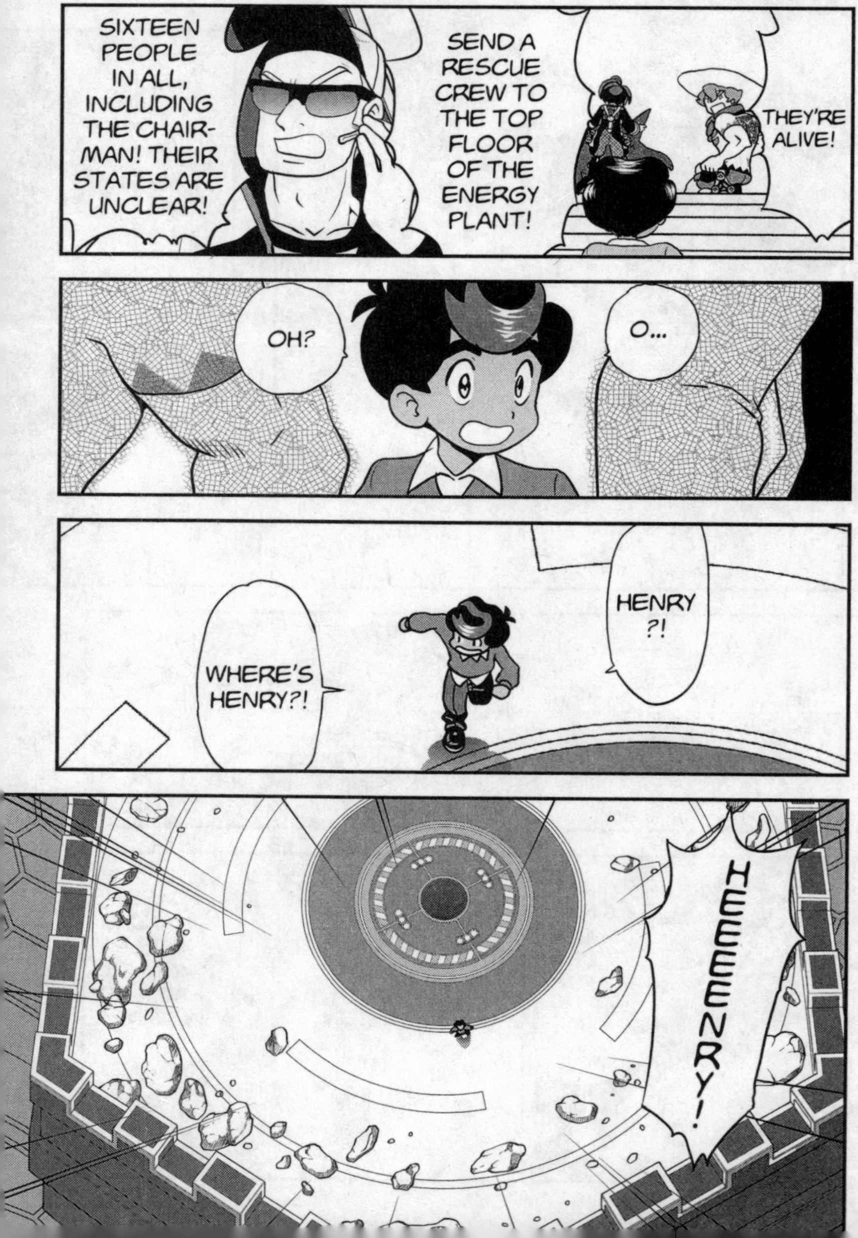
THEY'RE ALIVE!
SEND A RESCUE CREW TO THE TOP FLOOR OF THE ENERGY PLANT!
SIXTEEN PEOPLE IN ALL, INCLUDING THE CHAIR-MAN! THEIR STATES ARE UNCLEAR!
O...
OH?
HENRY ?!
WHERE'S HENRY?!
HEEEENRY!

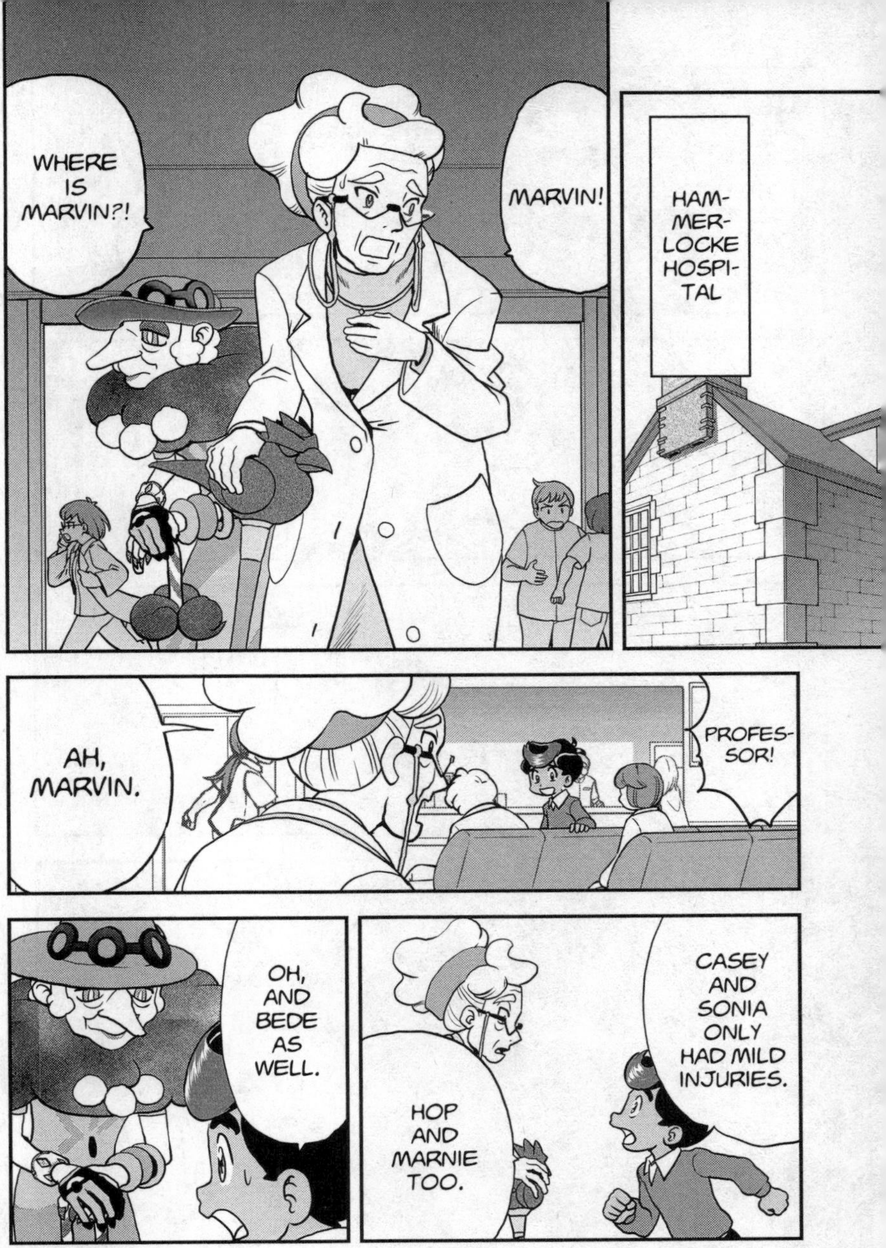
HAMMERLOCKE HOSPITAL
MARVIN!
WHERE IS MARVIN?!
PROFESSOR!
AH, MARVIN.
CASEY AND SONIA ONLY HAD MILD INJURIES.
HOP AND MARNIE TOO.
OH, AND BEDE AS WELL.

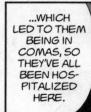

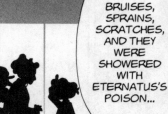

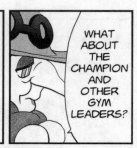

WHAT ABOUT THE CHAMPION AND OTHER GYM LEADERS?
BRUISES, SPRAINS, SCRATCHES, AND THEY WERE SHOWERED WITH ETERNATUS'S POISON...
...WHICH LED TO THEM BEING IN COMAS, SO THEY'VE ALL BEEN HOS-PITALIZED HERE.
CHAIRMAN ROSE, SORDWARD, AND SHIELBERT ARE PRIME SUSPECTS IN THE CASE...
...SO THEY HAVE BEEN HOSPITAL-IZED UNDER POLICE SUR-VEILLANCE. OLEANA, WHO WASN'T INJURED MUCH, IS WITH HIM.
SONIA AND THE OTHERS HAVE MOVED TO THE GREENROOM IN HAMMER-LOCKE STADIUM.
I'LL TAKE YOU THERE.
I'LL GO VISIT THE YOUNG ONES.
I'M GLAD EVERY-ONE'S OKAY.
ACTU-ALLY...
HEEEEEEEENRY!!

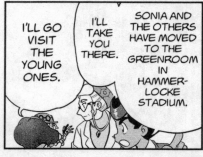

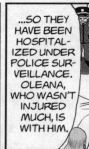

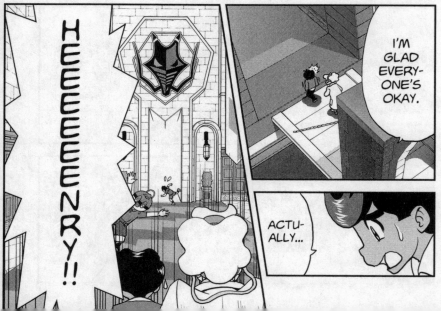

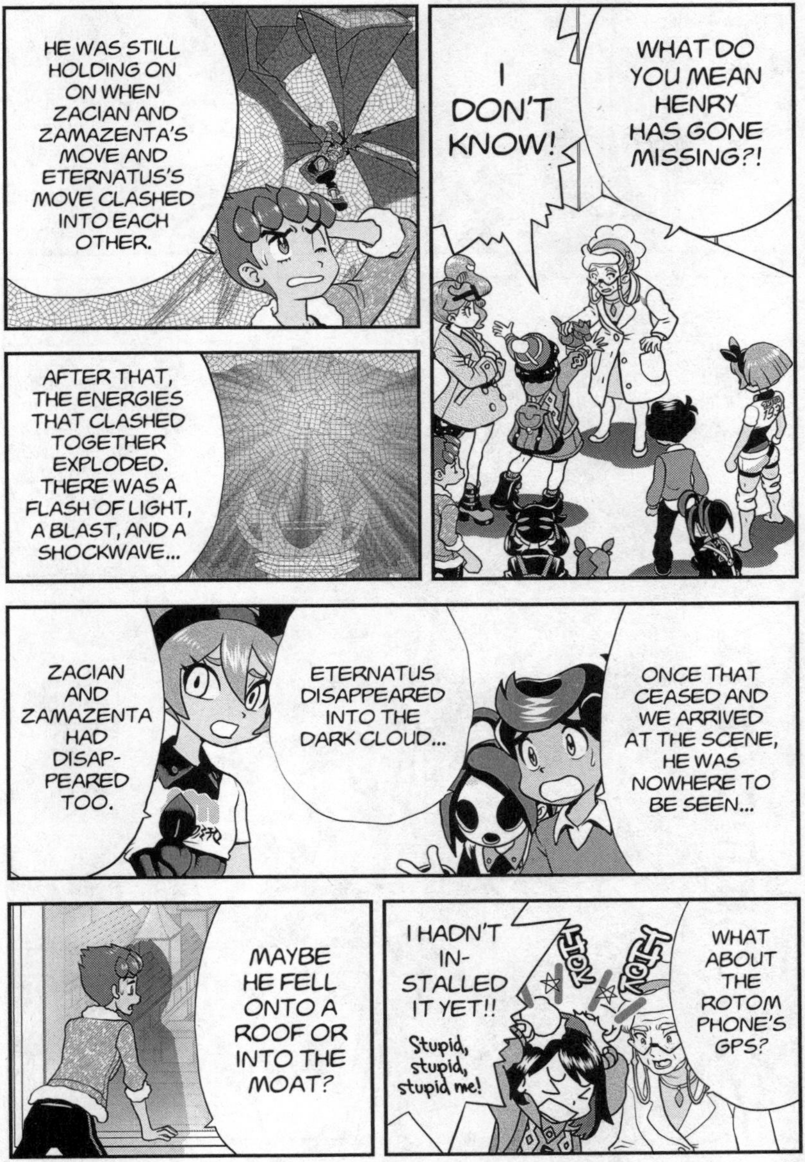

WHAT DO YOU MEAN HENRY HAS GONE MISSING?!
I DON'T KNOW!
HE WAS STILL HOLDING ON ON WHEN ZACIAN AND ZAMAZENTA'S MOVE AND ETERNATUS'S MOVE CLASHED INTO EACH OTHER.
AFTER THAT, THE ENERGIES THAT CLASHED TOGETHER EXPLODED. THERE WAS A FLASH OF LIGHT, A BLAST, AND A SHOCKWAVE...
ONCE THAT CEASED AND WE ARRIVED AT THE SCENE, HE WAS NOWHERE TO BE SEEN...
ETERNATUS DISAPPEARED INTO THE DARK CLOUD...
ZACIAN AND ZAMAZENTA HAD DISAP-PEARED TOO.
WHAT ABOUT THE ROTOM PHONE'S GPS?
I HADN'T IN-STALLED IT YET!!
Stupid, stupid, stupid me!
MAYBE HE FELL ONTO A ROOF OR INTO THE MOAT?

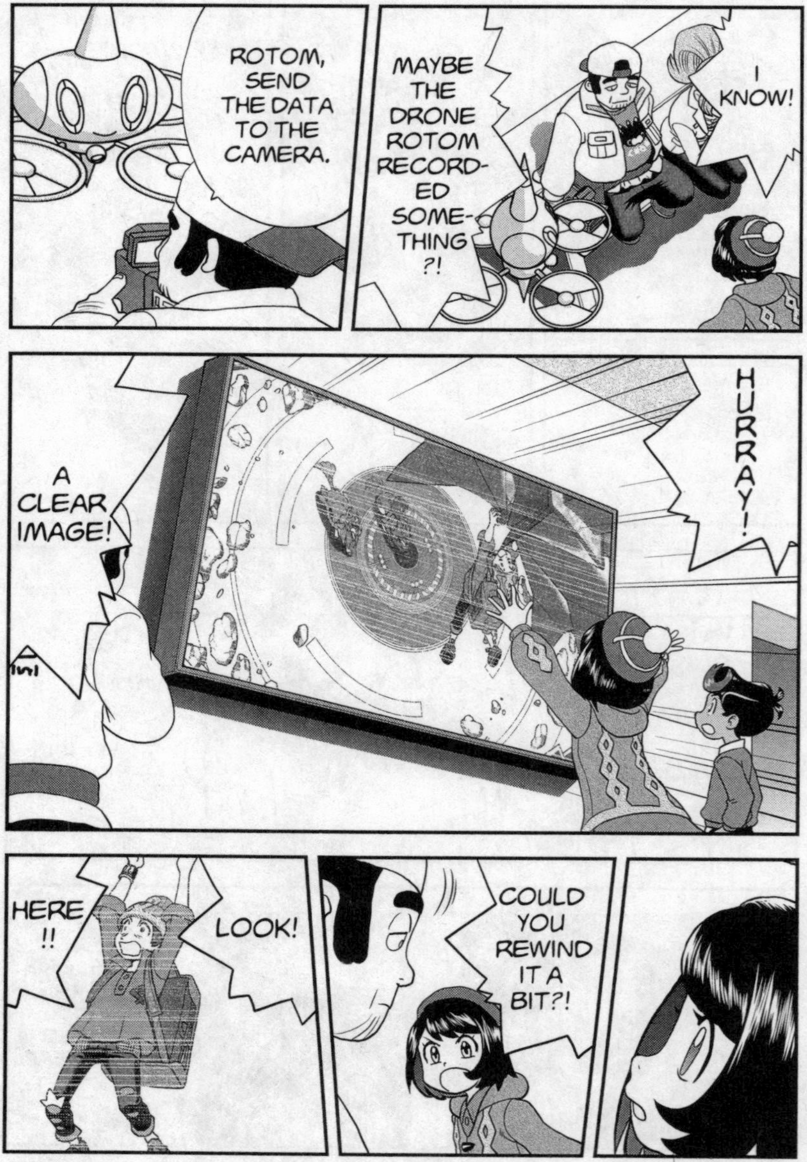
I KNOW!
MAYBE THE DRONE ROTOM RECORD-ED SOME-THING?!
ROTOM, SEND THE DATA TO THE CAMERA.
HURRAY!
A CLEAR IMAGE!
COULD YOU REWIND IT A BIT?!
LOOK!
HERE!!

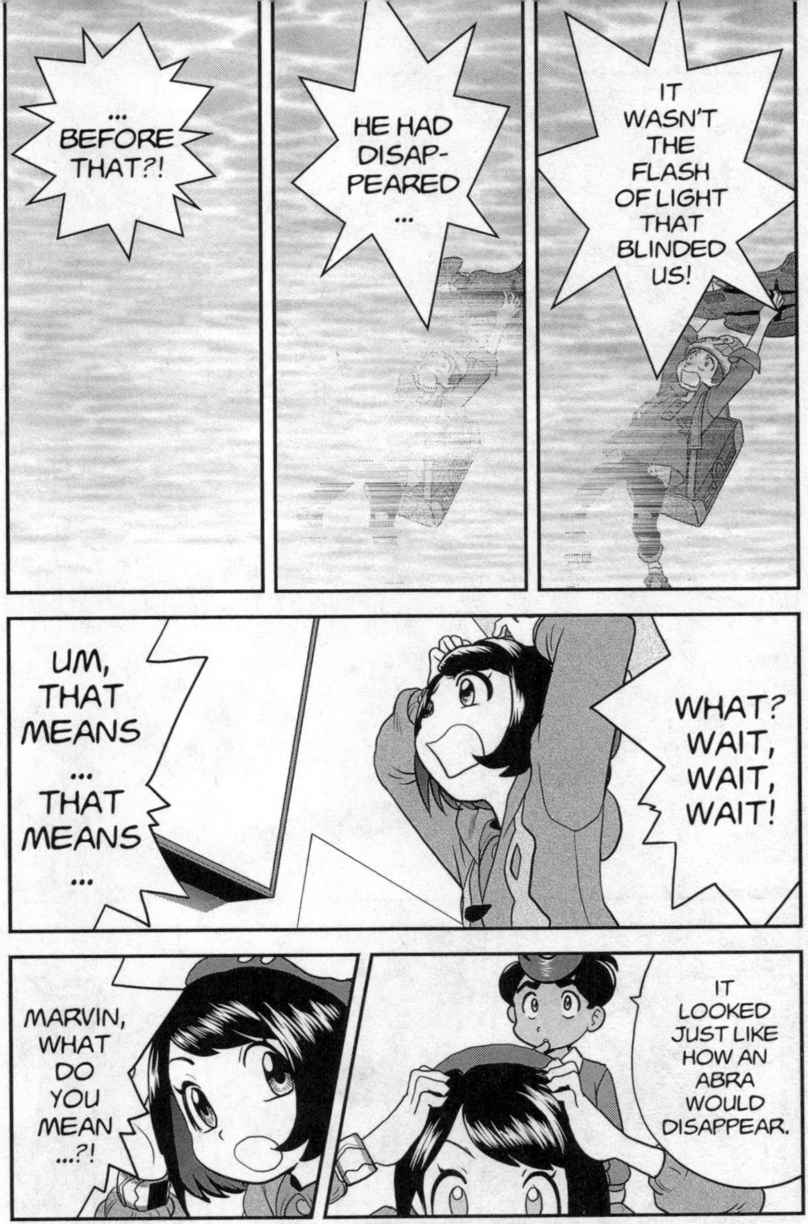
IT WASN'T THE FLASH OF LIGHT THAT BLINDED US!
HE HAD DISAP-PEARED ...
... BEFORE THAT?!
WHAT? WAIT, WAIT, WAIT!
UM, THAT MEANS ... THAT MEANS ...
IT LOOKED JUST LIKE HOW AN ABRA WOULD DISAPPEAR.
MARVIN, WHAT DO YOU MEAN ...?!

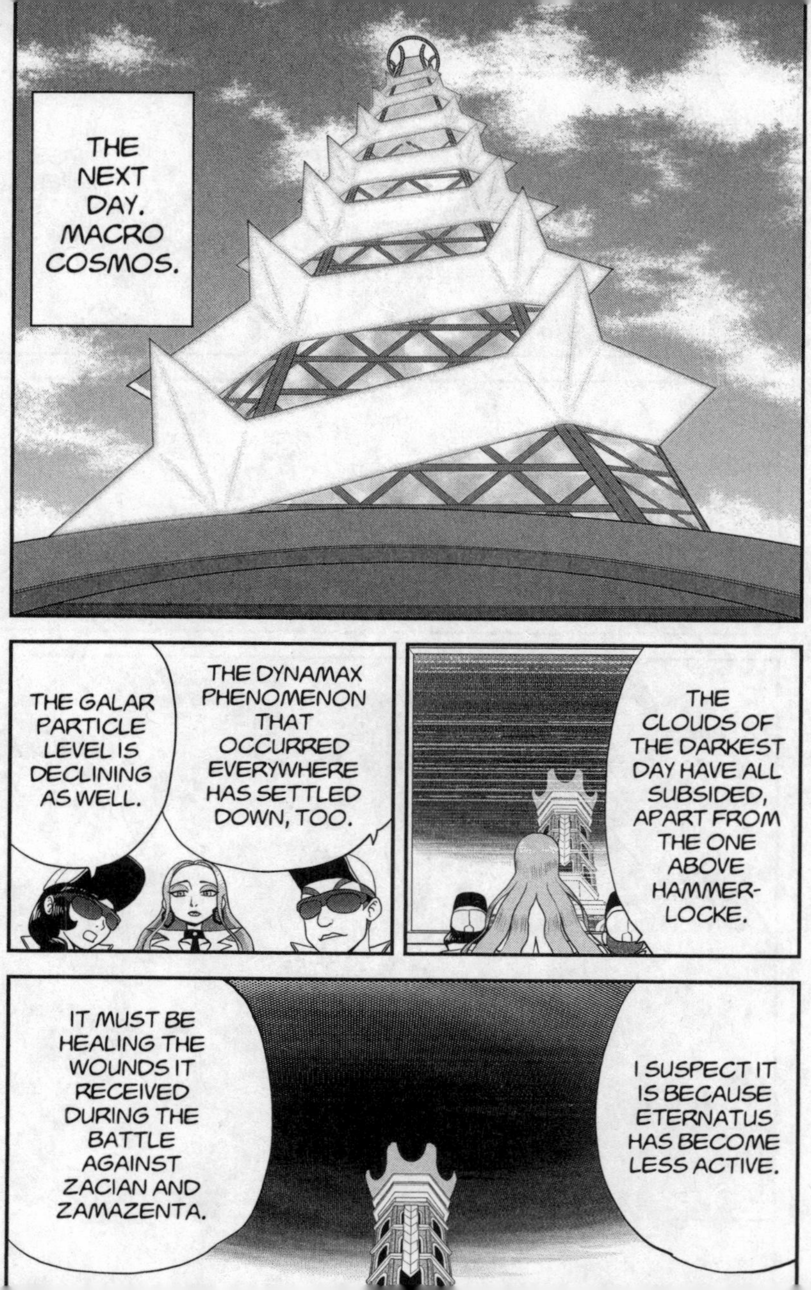
THE NEXT DAY. MACRO COSMOS.
THE CLOUDS OF THE DARKEST DAY HAVE ALL SUBSIDED, APART FROM THE ONE ABOVE HAMMER-LOCKE.
THE DYNAMAX PHENOMENON THAT OCCURRED EVERYWHERE HAS SETTLED DOWN, TOO.
THE GALAR PARTICLE LEVEL IS DECLINING AS WELL.
I SUSPECT IT IS BECAUSE ETERNATUS HAS BECOME LESS ACTIVE.
IT MUST BE HEALING THE WOUNDS IT RECEIVED DURING THE BATTLE AGAINST ZACIAN AND ZAMAZENTA.

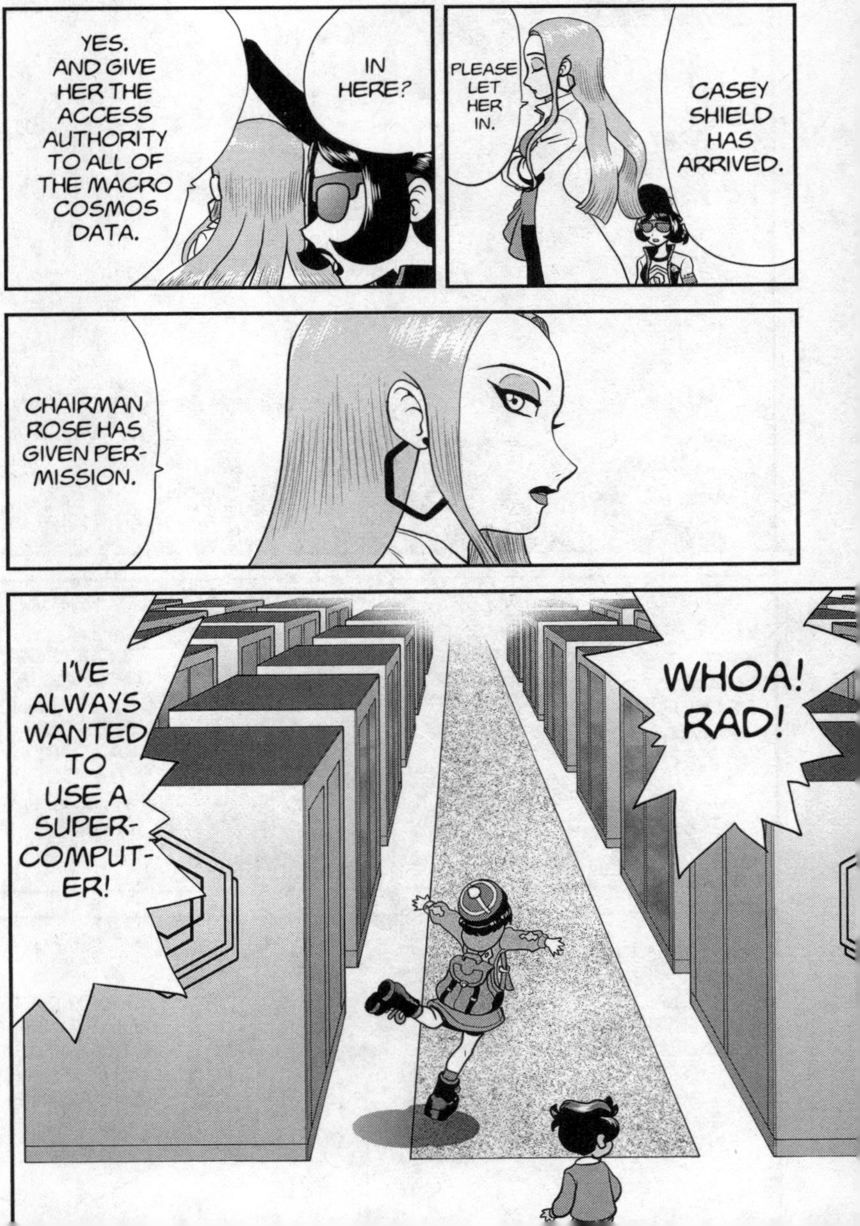
CASEY SHIELD HAS ARRIVED.
PLEASE LET HER IN.
IN HERE?
YES. AND GIVE HER THE ACCESS AUTHORITY TO ALL OF THE MACRO COSMOS DATA.
CHAIRMAN ROSE HAS GIVEN PER-MISSION.
WHOA! RAD!
I'VE ALWAYS WANTED TO USE A SUPER-COMPUT-ER!

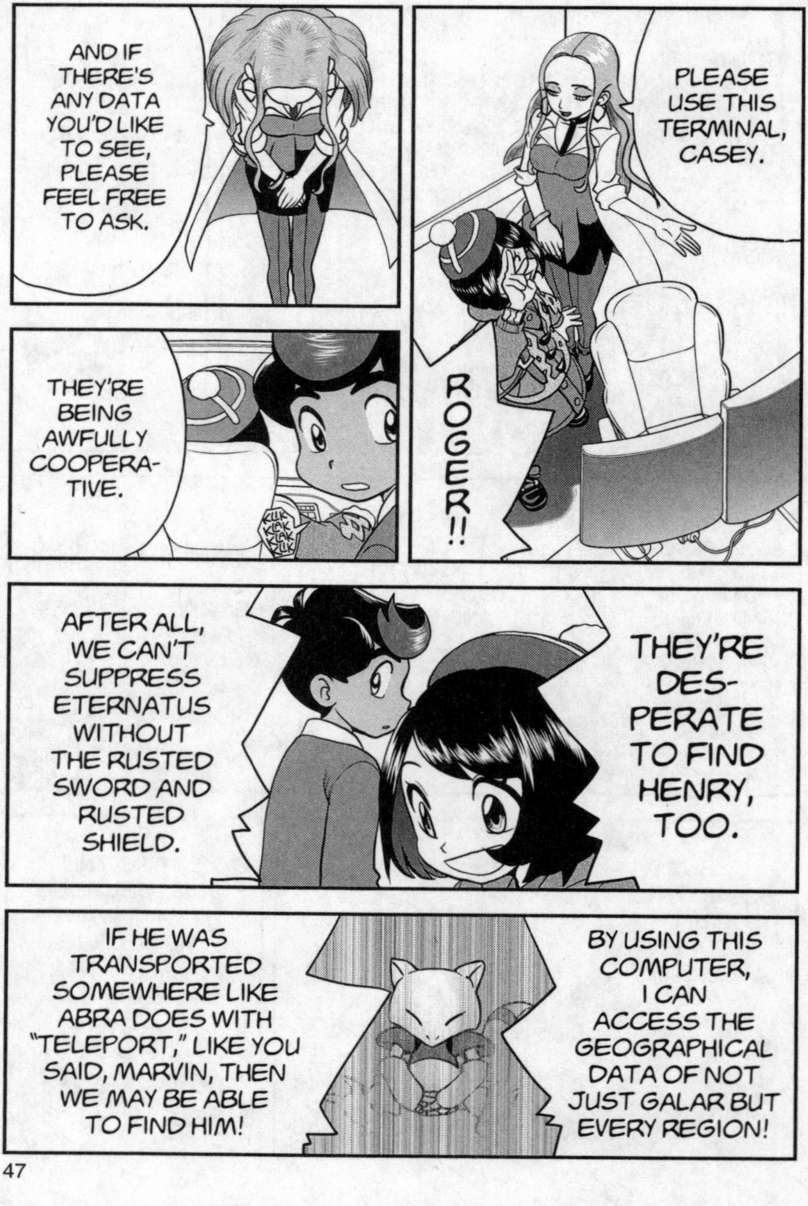
PLEASE USE THIS TERMINAL, CASEY.
ROGER!!
AND IF THERE'S ANY DATA YOU'D LIKE TO SEE, PLEASE FEEL FREE TO ASK.
THEY'RE BEING AWFULLY COOPERA-TIVE.
KLIK KLAK KLAK KLIK
THEY'RE DES-PERATE TO FIND HENRY, TOO.
AFTER ALL, WE CAN'T SUPPRESS ETERNATUS WITHOUT THE RUSTED SWORD AND RUSTED SHIELD.
BY USING THIS COMPUTER, I CAN ACCESS THE GEOGRAPHICAL DATA OF NOT JUST GALAR BUT EVERY REGION!
IF HE WAS TRANSPORTED SOMEWHERE LIKE ABRA DOES WITH "TELEPORT," LIKE YOU SAID, MARVIN, THEN WE MAY BE ABLE TO FIND HIM!

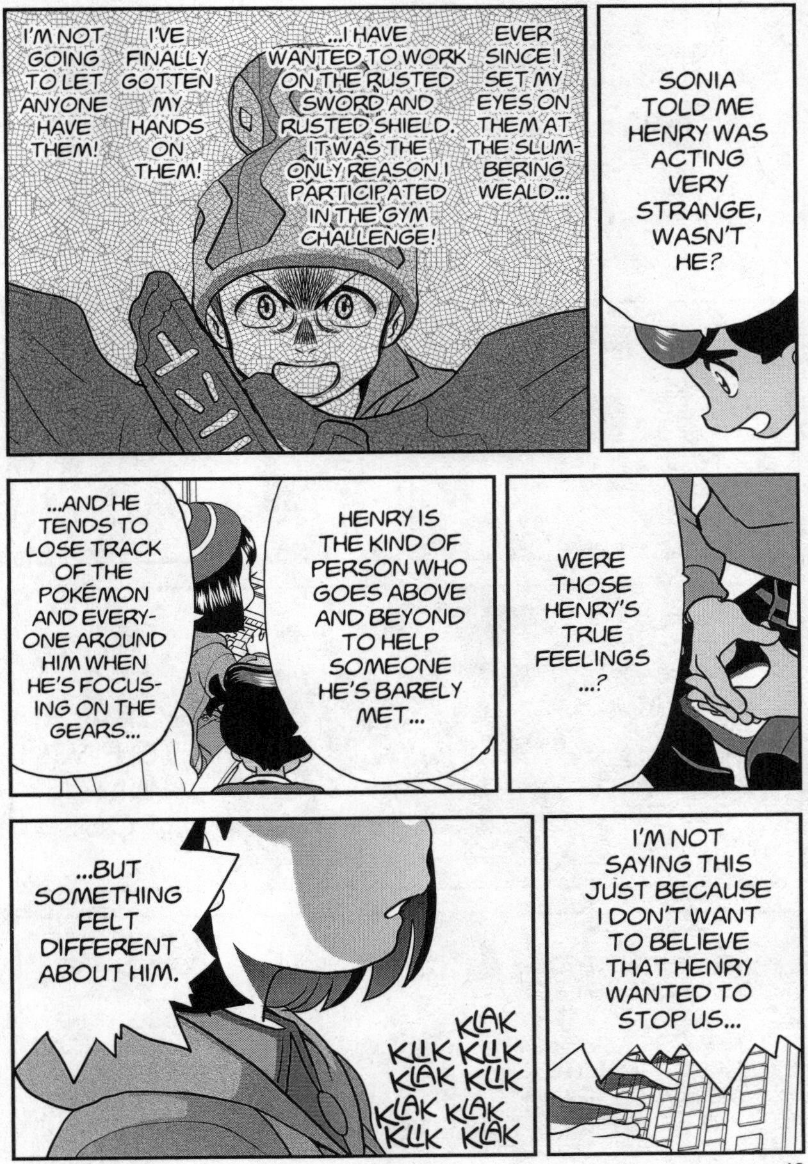
SONIA TOLD ME HENRY WAS ACTING VERY STRANGE, WASN'T HE?
EVER SINCE I SET MY EYES ON THEM AT THE SLUMBERING WEALD...
...I HAVE WANTED TO WORK ON THE RUSTED SWORD AND RUSTED SHIELD. IT WAS THE ONLY REASON I PARTICIPATED IN THE GYM CHALLENGE!
I'VE FINALLY GOTTEN MY HANDS ON THEM!
I'M NOT GOING TO LET ANYONE HAVE THEM!
WERE THOSE HENRY'S TRUE FEELINGS ...?
HENRY IS THE KIND OF PERSON WHO GOES ABOVE AND BEYOND TO HELP SOMEONE HE'S BARELY MET...
...AND HE TENDS TO LOSE TRACK OF THE POKÉMON AND EVERYONE AROUND HIM WHEN HE'S FOCUSING ON THE GEARS...
I'M NOT SAYING THIS JUST BECAUSE I DON'T WANT TO BELIEVE THAT HENRY WANTED TO STOP US...
...BUT SOMETHING FELT DIFFERENT ABOUT HIM.
KLAK KLIK KLIK KLAK KLIK KLAK KLAK KLAK KLIK KLIK KLAK

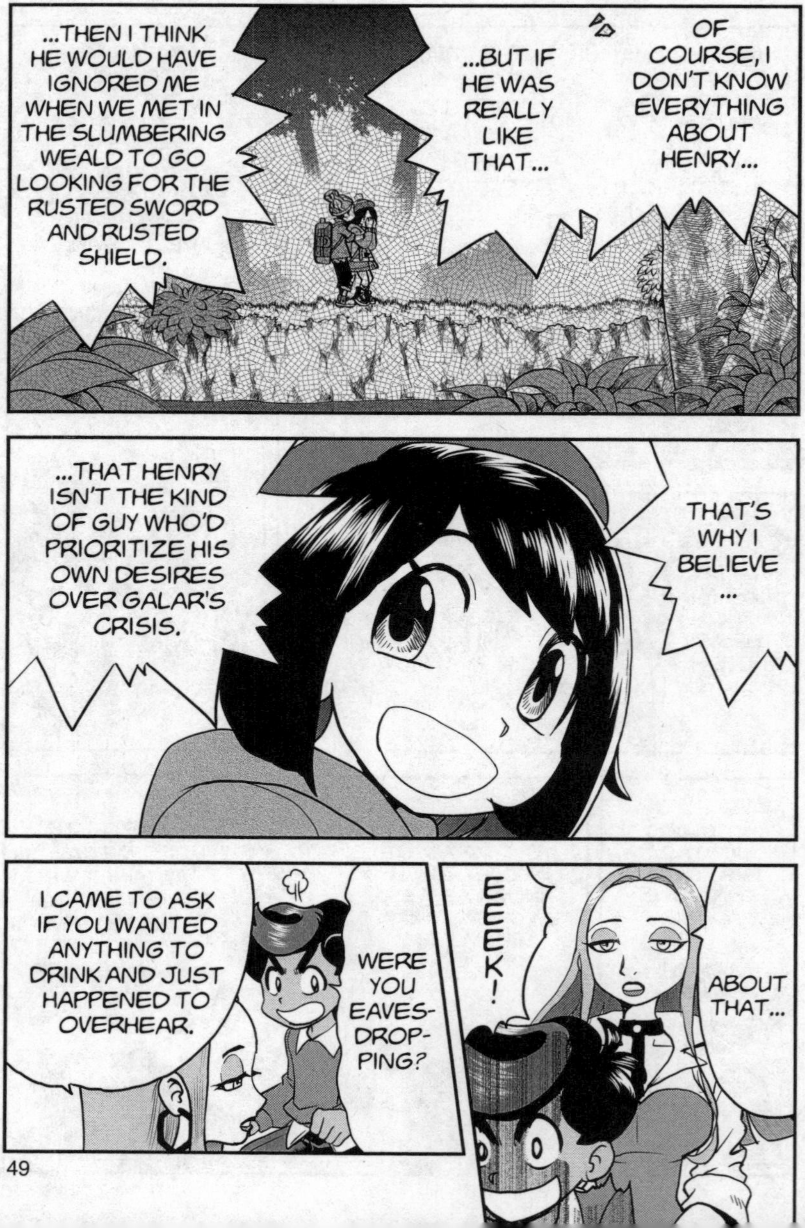
OF COURSE, I DON'T KNOW EVERYTHING ABOUT HENRY...
...BUT IF HE WAS REALLY LIKE THAT...
...THEN I THINK HE WOULD HAVE IGNORED ME WHEN WE MET IN THE SLUMBERING WEALD TO GO LOOKING FOR THE RUSTED SWORD AND RUSTED SHIELD.
THAT'S WHY I BELIEVE ...
...THAT HENRY ISN'T THE KIND OF GUY WHO'D PRIORITIZE HIS OWN DESIRES OVER GALAR'S CRISIS.
ABOUT THAT...
EEEEK!
WERE YOU EAVES-DROP-PING?
I CAME TO ASK IF YOU WANTED ANYTHING TO DRINK AND JUST HAPPENED TO OVERHEAR.

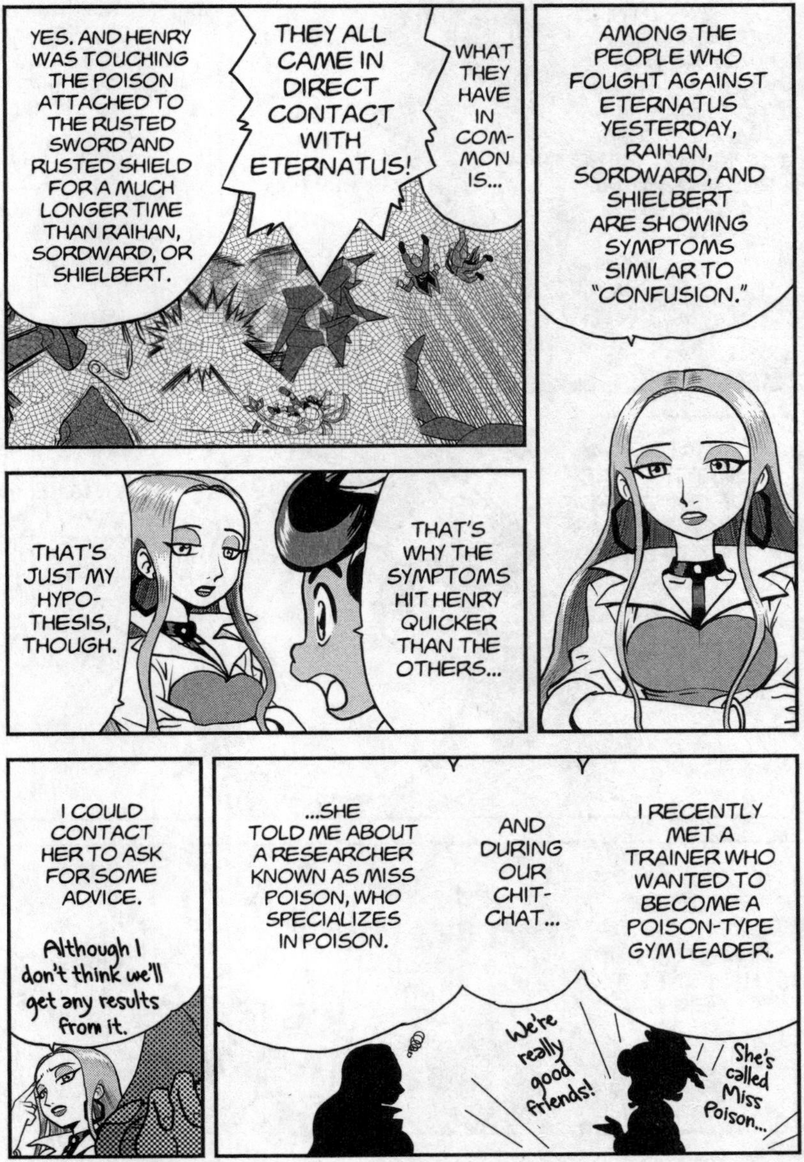
AMONG THE PEOPLE WHO FOUGHT AGAINST ETERNATUS YESTERDAY, RAIHAN, SORDWARD, AND SHIELBERT ARE SHOWING SYMPTOMS SIMILAR TO "CONFUSION."
WHAT THEY HAVE IN COM-MON IS...
THEY ALL CAME IN DIRECT CONTACT WITH ETERNATUS!
YES. AND HENRY WAS TOUCHING THE POISON ATTACHED TO THE RUSTED SWORD AND RUSTED SHIELD FOR A MUCH LONGER TIME THAN RAIHAN, SORDWARD, OR SHIELBERT.
THAT'S WHY THE SYMPTOMS HIT HENRY QUICKER THAN THE OTHERS...
THAT'S JUST MY HYPO-THESIS, THOUGH.
I RECENTLY MET A TRAINER WHO WANTED TO BECOME A POISON-TYPE GYM LEADER.
AND DURING OUR CHIT-CHAT...
...SHE TOLD ME ABOUT A RESEARCHER KNOWN AS MISS POISON, WHO SPECIALIZES IN POISON.
She's called Miss Poison...
We're really good friends!
I COULD CONTACT HER TO ASK FOR SOME ADVICE.
Although I don't think we'll get any results from it.

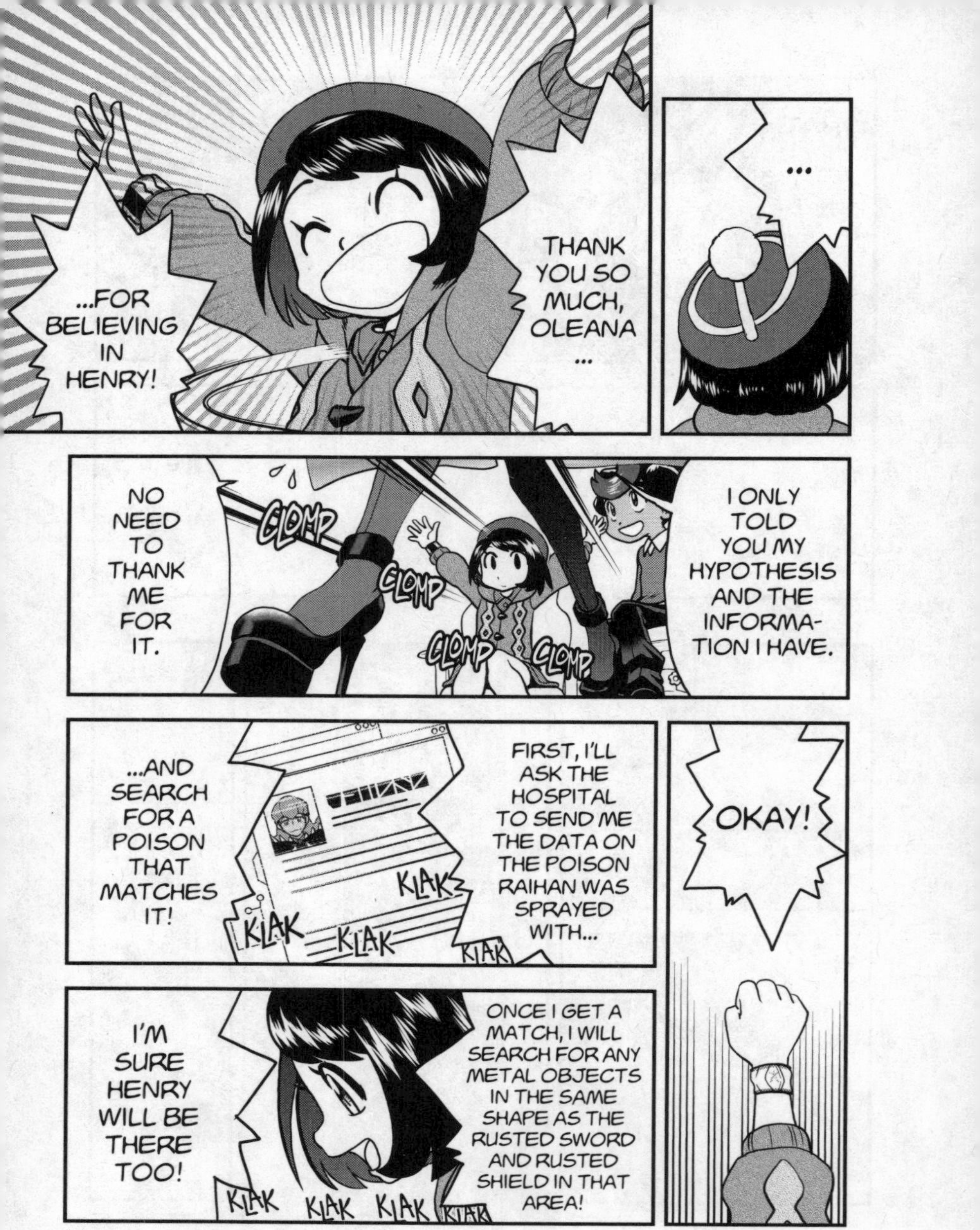
...
THANK YOU SO MUCH, OLEANA ...
...FOR BELIEVING IN HENRY!
I ONLY TOLD YOU MY HYPOTHESIS AND THE INFORMA-TION I HAVE.
CLOMP CLOMP CLOMP CLOMP
NO NEED TO THANK ME FOR IT.
OKAY!
FIRST, I'LL ASK THE HOSPITAL TO SEND ME THE DATA ON THE POISON RAIHAN WAS SPRAYED WITH...
KLAK KLAK KLAK KLAK
...AND SEARCH FOR A POISON THAT MATCHES IT!
ONCE I GET A MATCH, I WILL SEARCH FOR ANY METAL OBJECTS IN THE SAME SHAPE AS THE RUSTED SWORD AND RUSTED SHIELD IN THAT AREA!
KLAK KLAK KLAK KLAK
I'M SURE HENRY WILL BE THERE TOO!

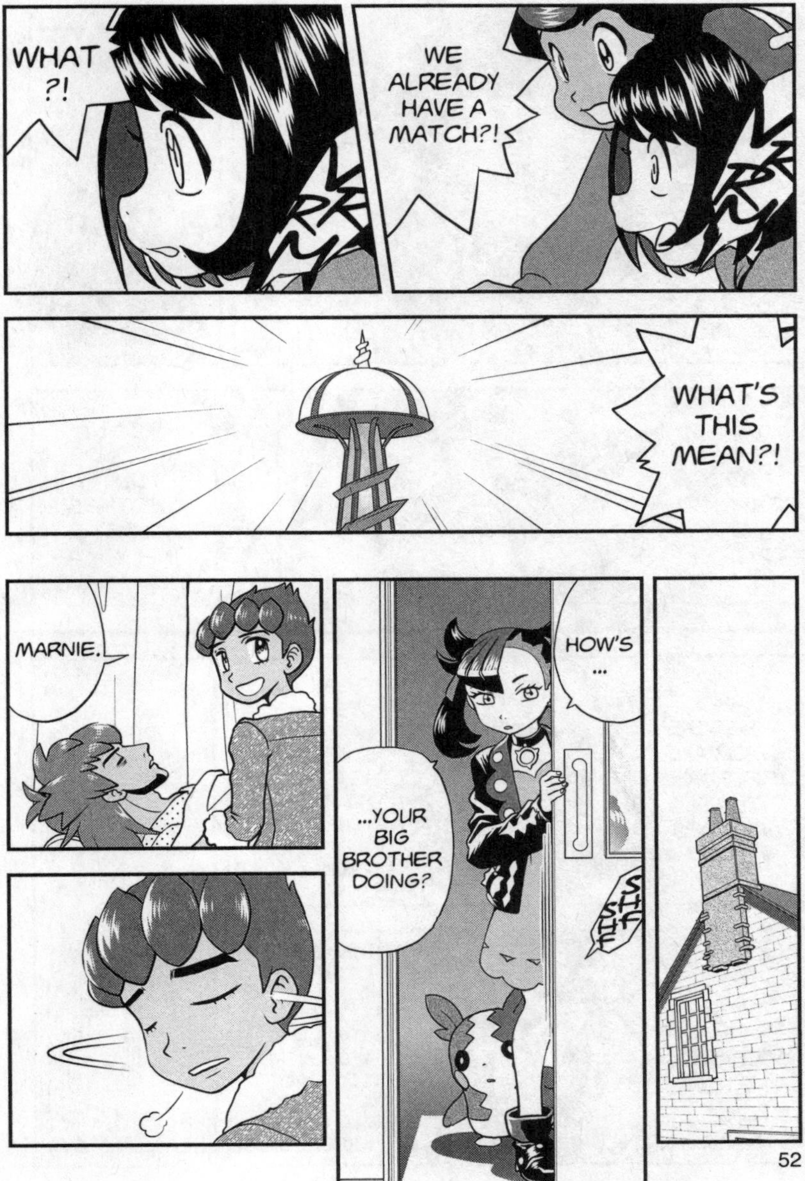
WE ALREADY HAVE A MATCH?!
WHAT ?!
WHAT'S THIS MEAN?!
HOW'S ...
...YOUR BIG BROTHER DOING?
SHF SHF
MARNIE.

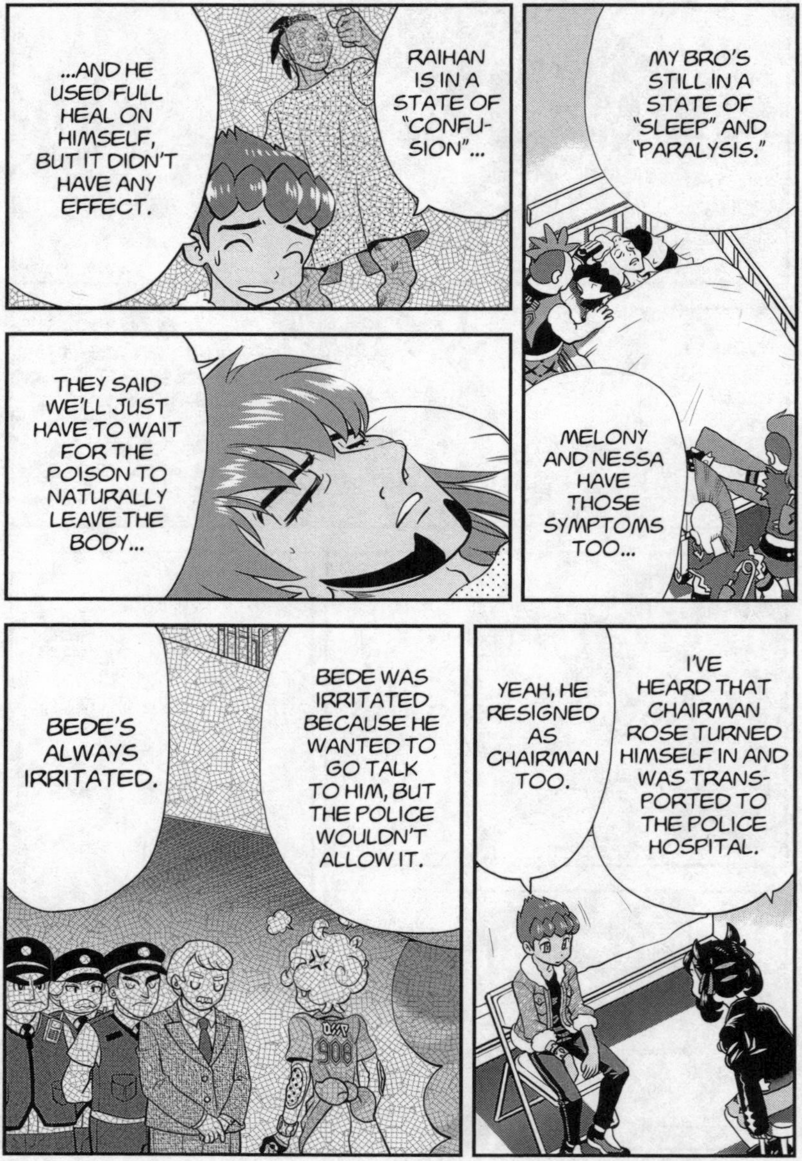
MY BRO'S STILL IN A STATE OF "SLEEP" AND "PARALYSIS."
MELONY AND NESSA HAVE THOSE SYMPTOMS TOO...
RAIHAN IS IN A STATE OF "CONFUSION"...
...AND HE USED FULL HEAL ON HIMSELF, BUT IT DIDN'T HAVE ANY EFFECT.
THEY SAID WE'LL JUST HAVE TO WAIT FOR THE POISON TO NATURALLY LEAVE THE BODY...
I'VE HEARD THAT CHAIRMAN ROSE TURNED HIMSELF IN AND WAS TRANSPORTED TO THE POLICE HOSPITAL.
YEAH, HE RESIGNED AS CHAIRMAN TOO.
BEDE WAS IRRITATED BECAUSE HE WANTED TO GO TALK TO HIM, BUT THE POLICE WOULDN'T ALLOW IT.
BEDE'S ALWAYS IRRITATED.

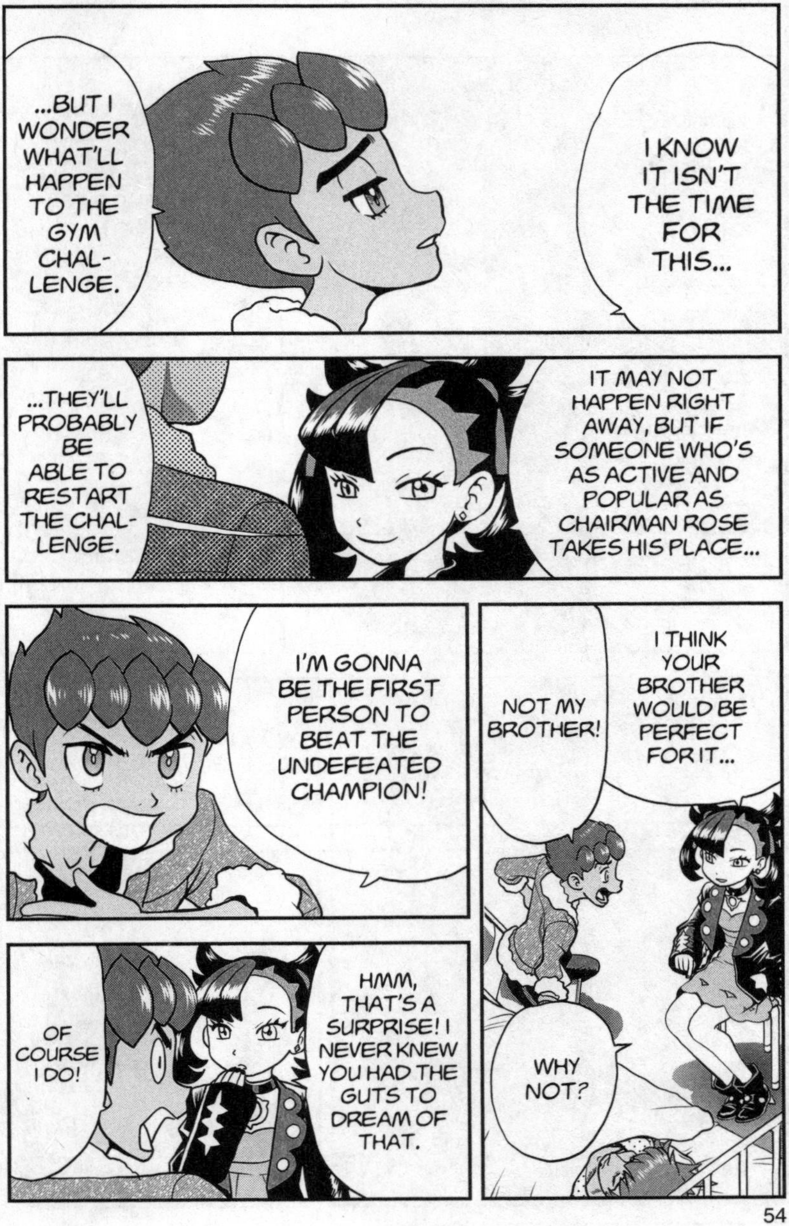
I KNOW IT ISN'T THE TIME FOR THIS...
...BUT I WONDER WHAT'LL HAPPEN TO THE GYM CHAL-LENGE.
IT MAY NOT HAPPEN RIGHT AWAY, BUT IF SOMEONE WHO'S AS ACTIVE AND POPULAR AS CHAIRMAN ROSE TAKES HIS PLACE...
...THEY'LL PROBABLY BE ABLE TO RESTART THE CHAL-LENGE.
I THINK YOUR BROTHER WOULD BE PERFECT FOR IT...
NOT MY BROTHER!
WHY NOT?
I'M GONNA BE THE FIRST PERSON TO BEAT THE UNDEFEATED CHAMPION!
HMM, THAT'S A SURPRISE! I NEVER KNEW YOU HAD THE GUTS TO DREAM OF THAT.
OF COURSE I DO!

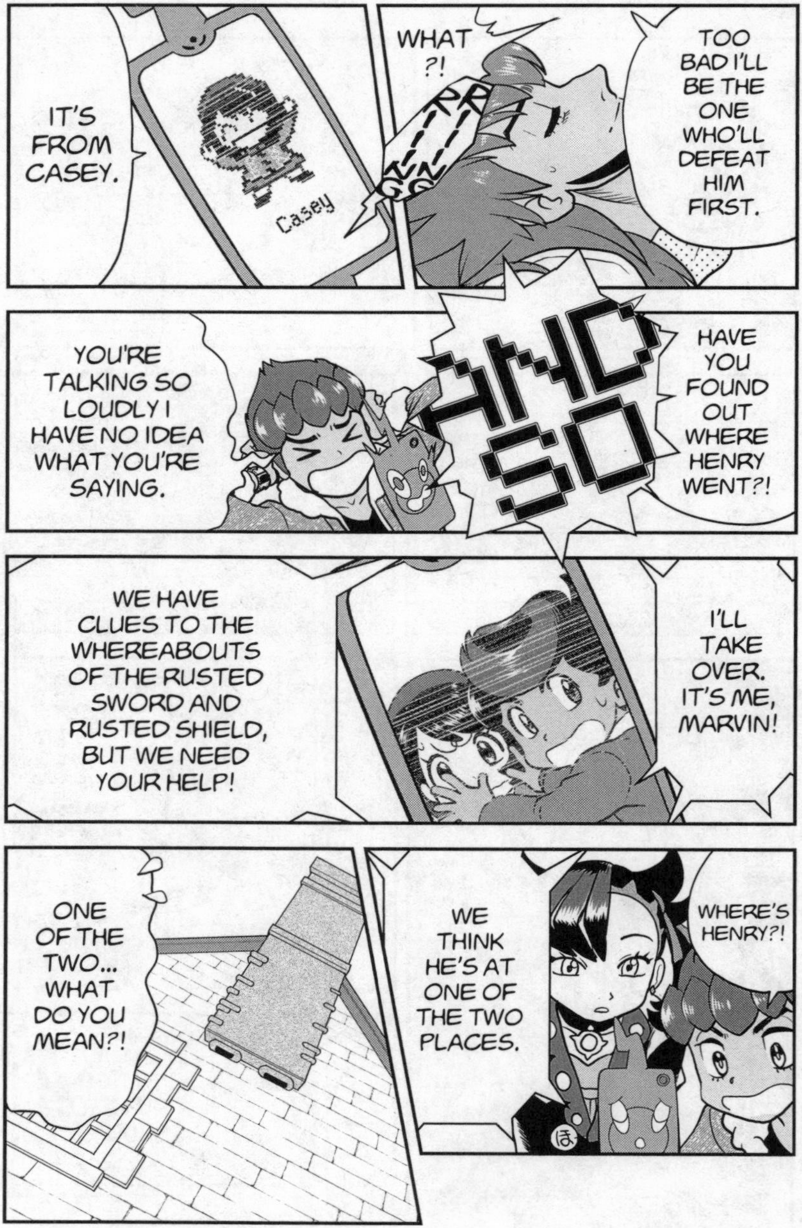
TOO BAD I'LL BE THE ONE WHO'LL DEFEAT HIM FIRST.
WHAT ?!
PRIIIIIINNGG
IT'S FROM CASEY.
Casey
HAVE YOU FOUND OUT WHERE HENRY WENT?!
AND SO
YOU'RE TALKING SO LOUDLY I HAVE NO IDEA WHAT YOU'RE SAYING.
I'LL TAKE OVER. IT'S ME, MARVIN!
WE HAVE CLUES TO THE WHEREABOUTS OF THE RUSTED SWORD AND RUSTED SHIELD, BUT WE NEED YOUR HELP!
WHERE'S HENRY?!
WE THINK HE'S AT ONE OF THE TWO PLACES.
ほ
ONE OF THE TWO... WHAT DO YOU MEAN?!

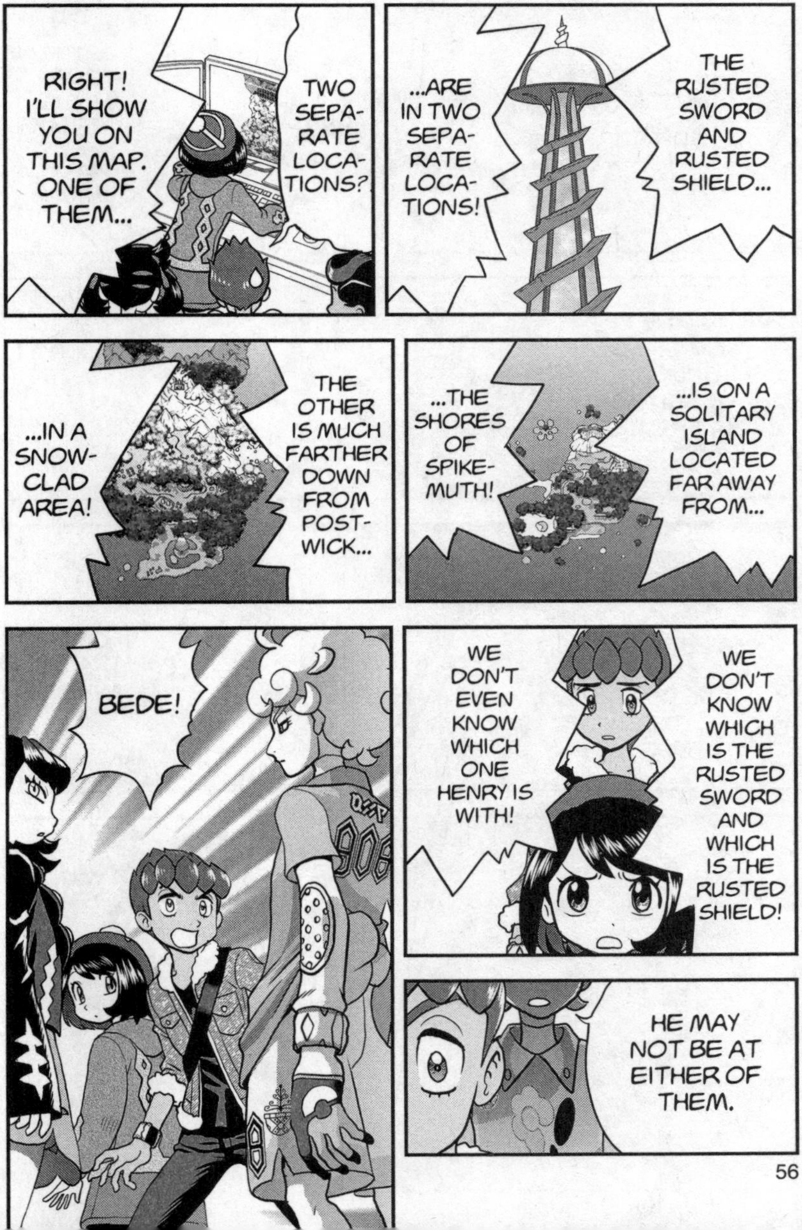
THE RUSTED SWORD AND RUSTED SHIELD...
...ARE IN TWO SEPARATE LOCATIONS!
TWO SEPARATE LOCATIONS?
RIGHT! I'LL SHOW YOU ON THIS MAP. ONE OF THEM...
...IS ON A SOLITARY ISLAND LOCATED FAR AWAY FROM...
...THE SHORES OF SPIKEMUTH!
THE OTHER IS MUCH FARTHER DOWN FROM POSTWICK...
...IN A SNOW-CLAD AREA!
WE DON'T KNOW WHICH IS THE RUSTED SWORD AND WHICH IS THE RUSTED SHIELD!
WE DON'T EVEN KNOW WHICH ONE HENRY IS WITH!
HE MAY NOT BE AT EITHER OF THEM.
BEDE!

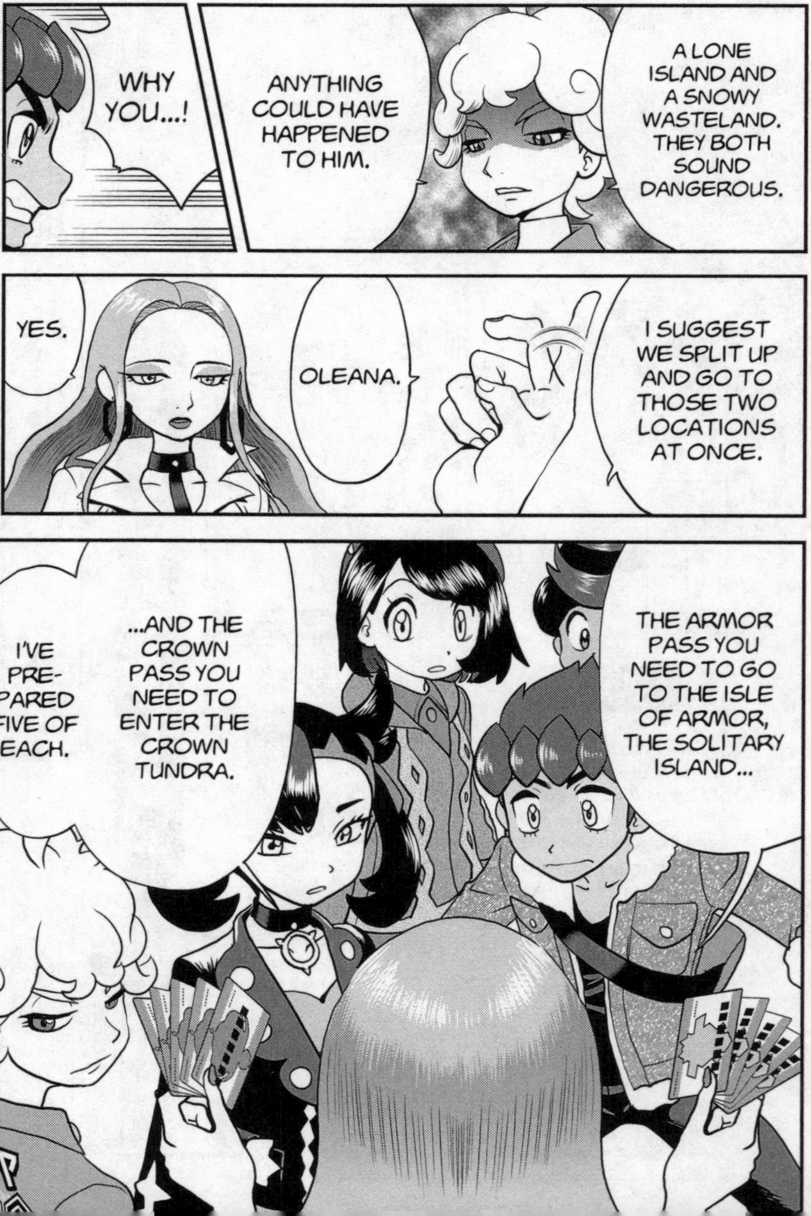
A LONE ISLAND AND A SNOWY WASTELAND. THEY BOTH SOUND DANGEROUS.
ANYTHING COULD HAVE HAPPENED TO HIM.
WHY YOU...!
I SUGGEST WE SPLIT UP AND GO TO THOSE TWO LOCATIONS AT ONCE.
OLEANA.
YES.
THE ARMOR PASS YOU NEED TO GO TO THE ISLE OF ARMOR, THE SOLITARY ISLAND...
...AND THE CROWN PASS YOU NEED TO ENTER THE CROWN TUNDRA.
I'VE PRE-PARED FIVE OF EACH.

GIGANTAMAX SNORLAX

TYPE	Normal
ABILITY	Immunity Thick Fat
G-MAX MOVE	G-Max Replenish

HEIGHT	114'10"+
WEIGHT	??? lbs

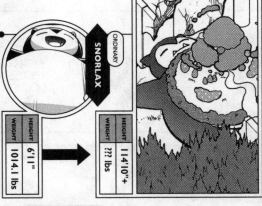

ORDINARY

SNORLAX

HEIGHT	6'11"
WEIGHT	1014.1 lbs

A Gigantamax Snorlax looks like a mountain, especially with the large tree in the center of its belly. Sometimes food scraps and berries will Gigantify along with Snorlax.

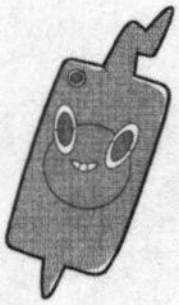

STRATEGY NOTES

The Normal-type move used by a Gigantamax Snorlax is G-Max Replenish. It is a unique move that regenerates the berries that Snorlax and even the team members ate. A single berry may settle the course of a battle between two skilled trainers, so you must not let your guard down!!

Adventure 31 Flutter!! Tickets to a New Land

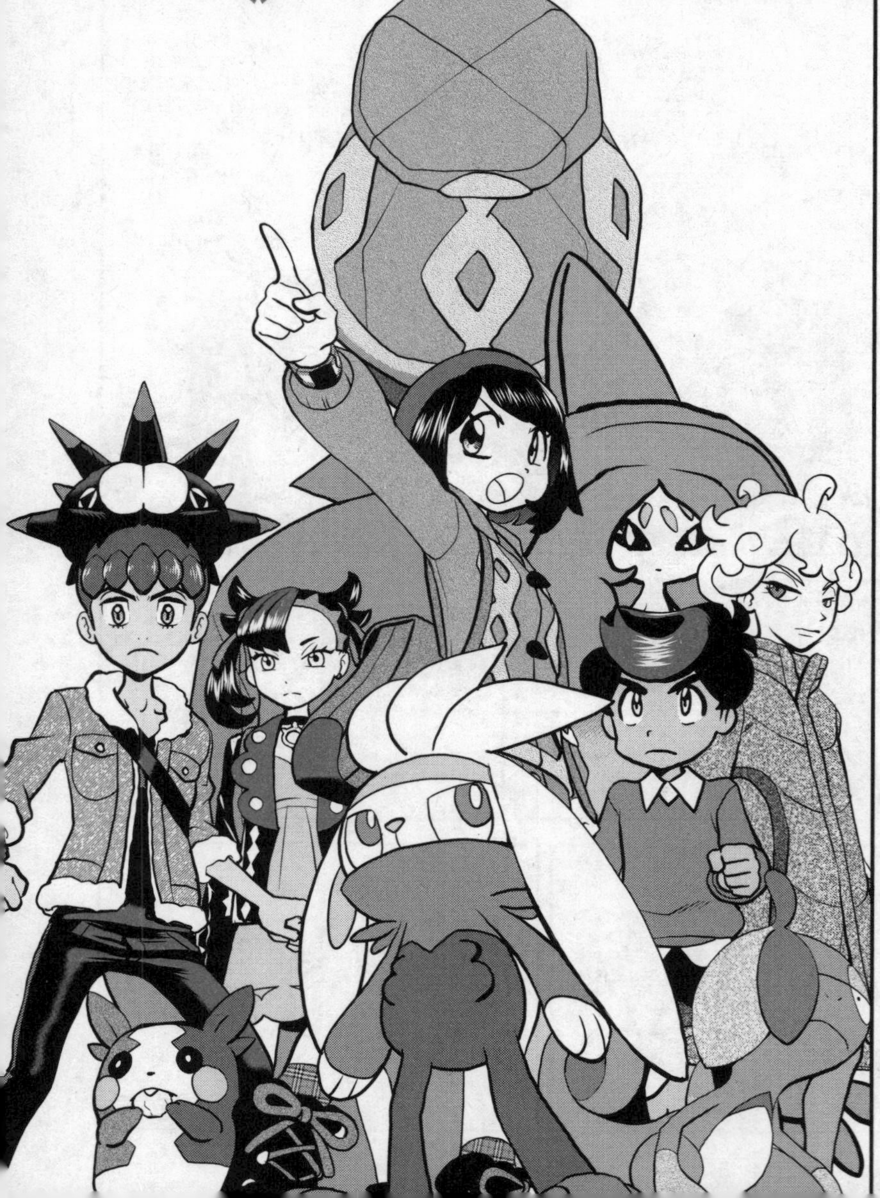

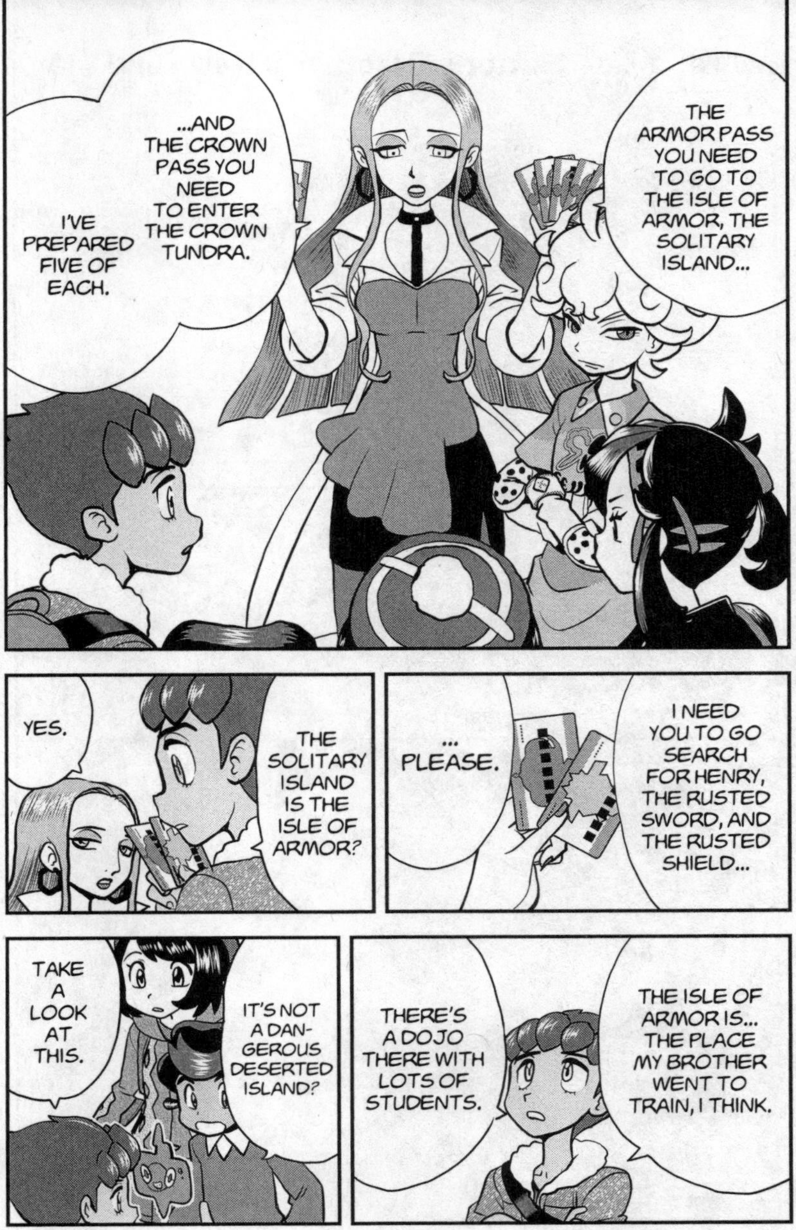
THE ARMOR PASS YOU NEED TO GO TO THE ISLE OF ARMOR, THE SOLITARY ISLAND...
...AND THE CROWN PASS YOU NEED TO ENTER THE CROWN TUNDRA.
I'VE PREPARED FIVE OF EACH.
I NEED YOU TO GO SEARCH FOR HENRY, THE RUSTED SWORD, AND THE RUSTED SHIELD...
...PLEASE.
THE SOLITARY ISLAND IS THE ISLE OF ARMOR?
YES.
THE ISLE OF ARMOR IS... THE PLACE MY BROTHER WENT TO TRAIN, I THINK.
THERE'S A DOJO THERE WITH LOTS OF STUDENTS.
IT'S NOT A DANGEROUS DESERTED ISLAND?
TAKE A LOOK AT THIS.

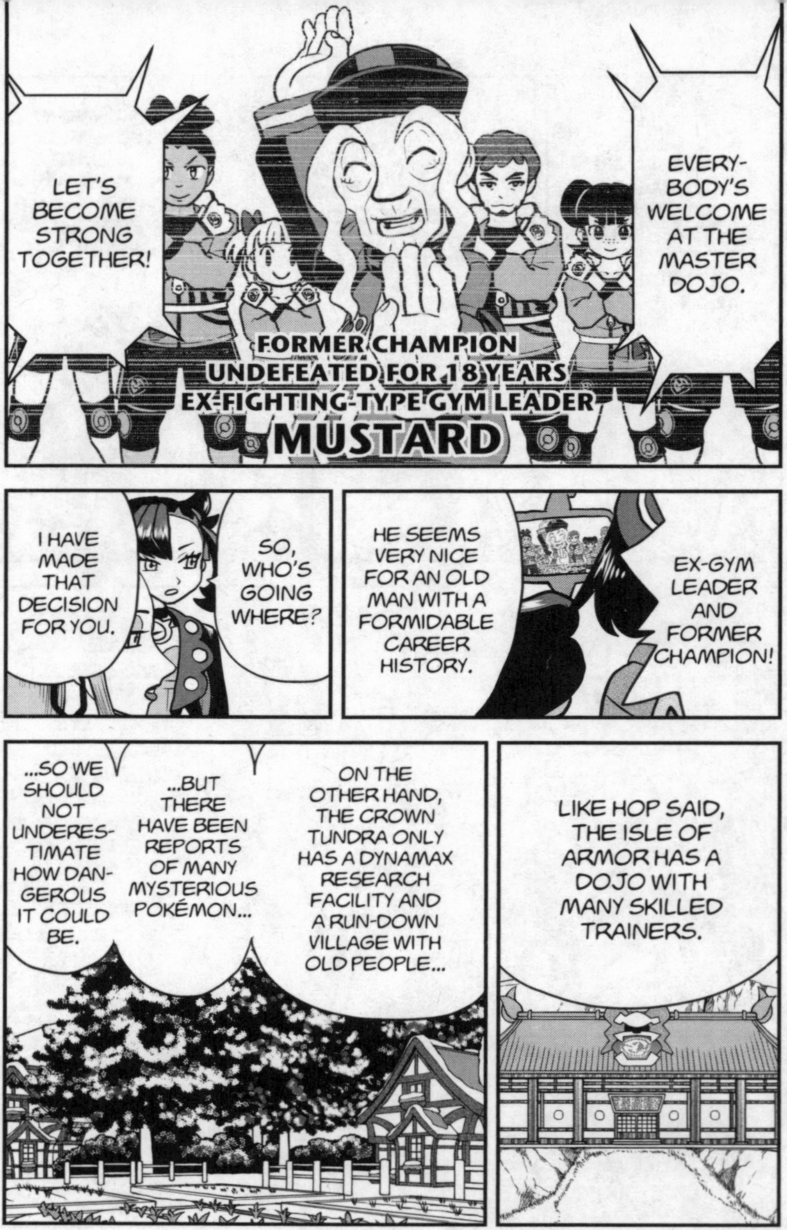
EVERY-BODY'S WELCOME AT THE MASTER DOJO.
LET'S BECOME STRONG TOGETHER!
FORMER CHAMPION
UNDEFEATED FOR 18 YEARS
EX-FIGHTING-TYPE GYM LEADER
MUSTARD
EX-GYM LEADER AND FORMER CHAMPION!
HE SEEMS VERY NICE FOR AN OLD MAN WITH A FORMIDABLE CAREER HISTORY.
SO, WHO'S GOING WHERE?
I HAVE MADE THAT DECISION FOR YOU.
LIKE HOP SAID, THE ISLE OF ARMOR HAS A DOJO WITH MANY SKILLED TRAINERS.
ON THE OTHER HAND, THE CROWN TUNDRA ONLY HAS A DYNAMAX RESEARCH FACILITY AND A RUN-DOWN VILLAGE WITH OLD PEOPLE...
...BUT THERE HAVE BEEN REPORTS OF MANY MYSTERIOUS POKÉMON...
...SO WE SHOULD NOT UNDERES-TIMATE HOW DAN-GEROUS IT COULD BE.

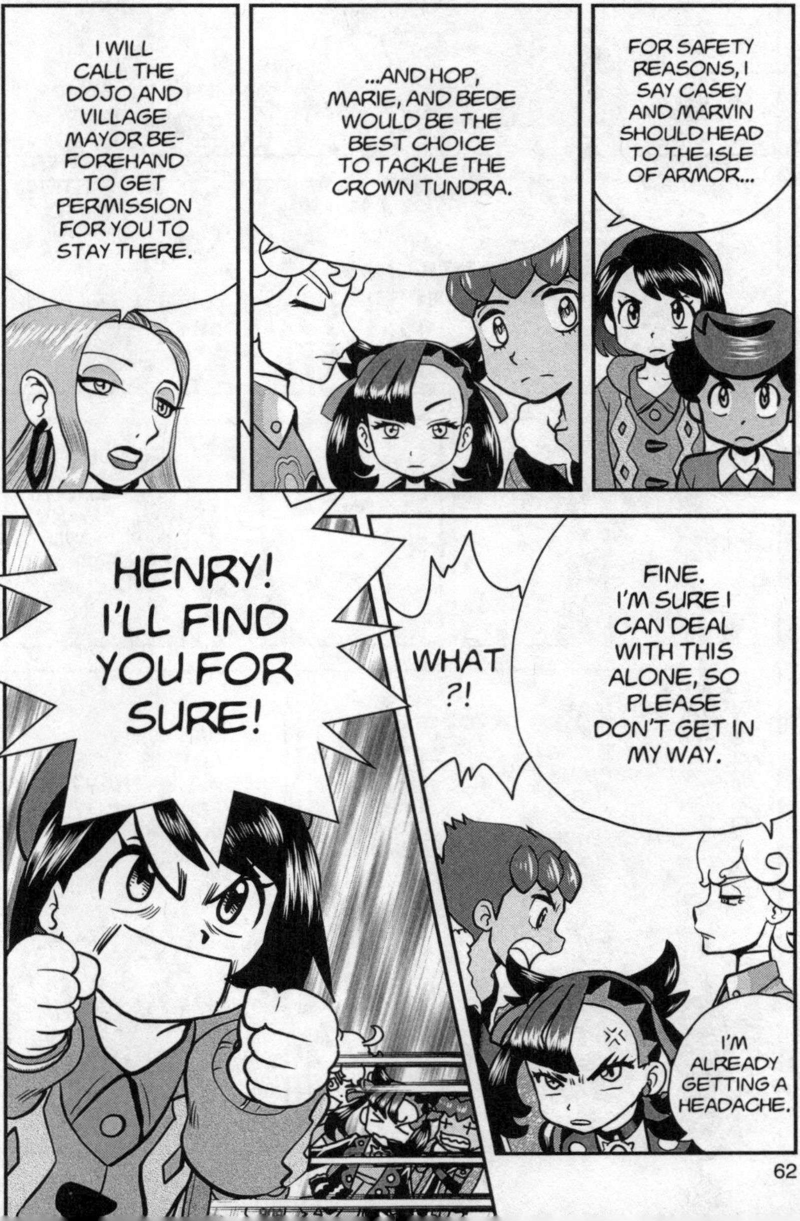
FOR SAFETY REASONS, I SAY CASEY AND MARVIN SHOULD HEAD TO THE ISLE OF ARMOR...
...AND HOP, MARIE, AND BEDE WOULD BE THE BEST CHOICE TO TACKLE THE CROWN TUNDRA.
I WILL CALL THE DOJO AND VILLAGE MAYOR BEFOREHAND TO GET PERMISSION FOR YOU TO STAY THERE.
FINE. I'M SURE I CAN DEAL WITH THIS ALONE, SO PLEASE DON'T GET IN MY WAY.
WHAT?!
I'M ALREADY GETTING A HEADACHE.
HENRY! I'LL FIND YOU FOR SURE!

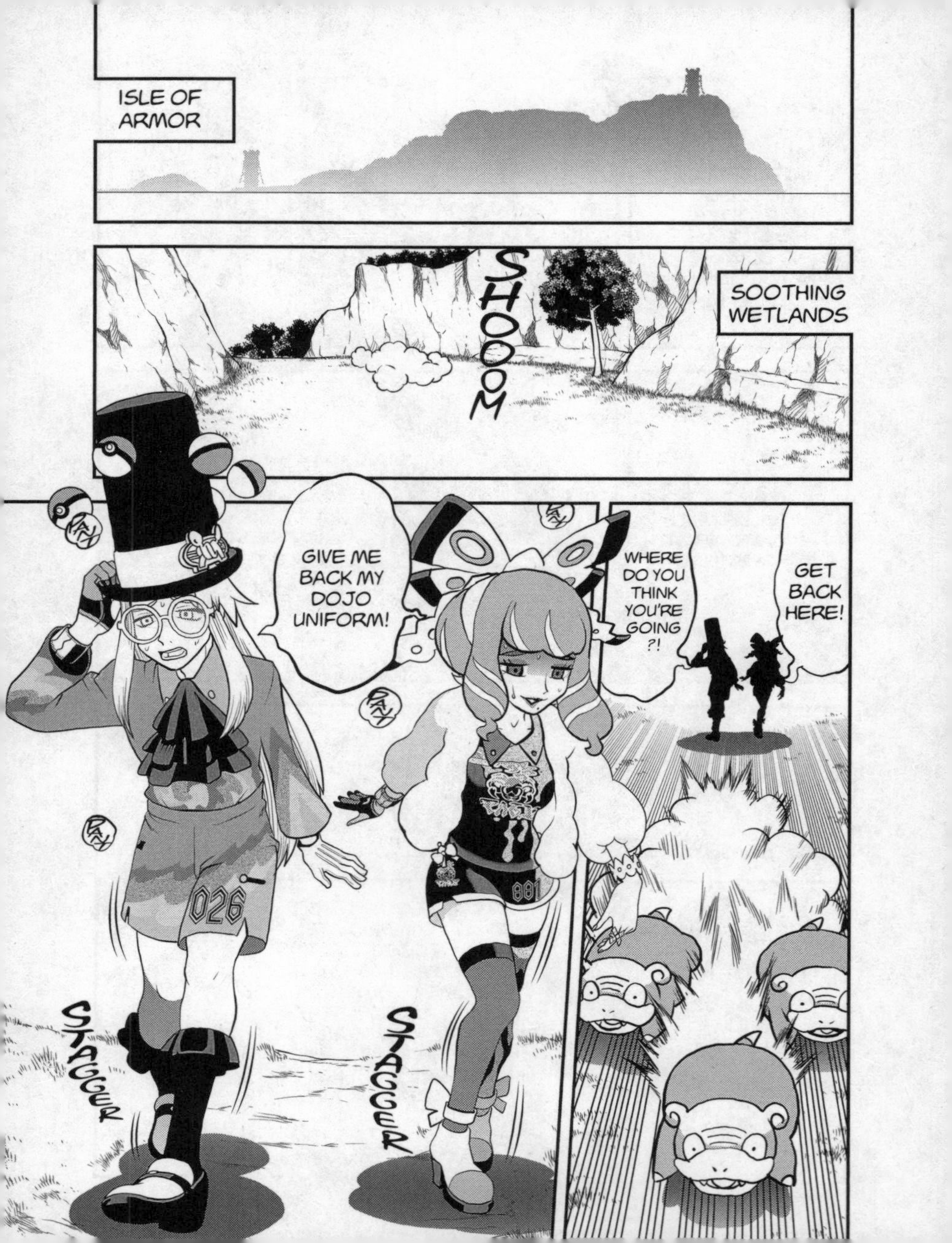
ISLE OF ARMOR
SOOTHING WETLANDS
SHOOOOM
GIVE ME BACK MY DOJO UNIFORM!
WHERE DO YOU THINK YOU'RE GOING ?!
GET BACK HERE!
STAGGER
STAGGER

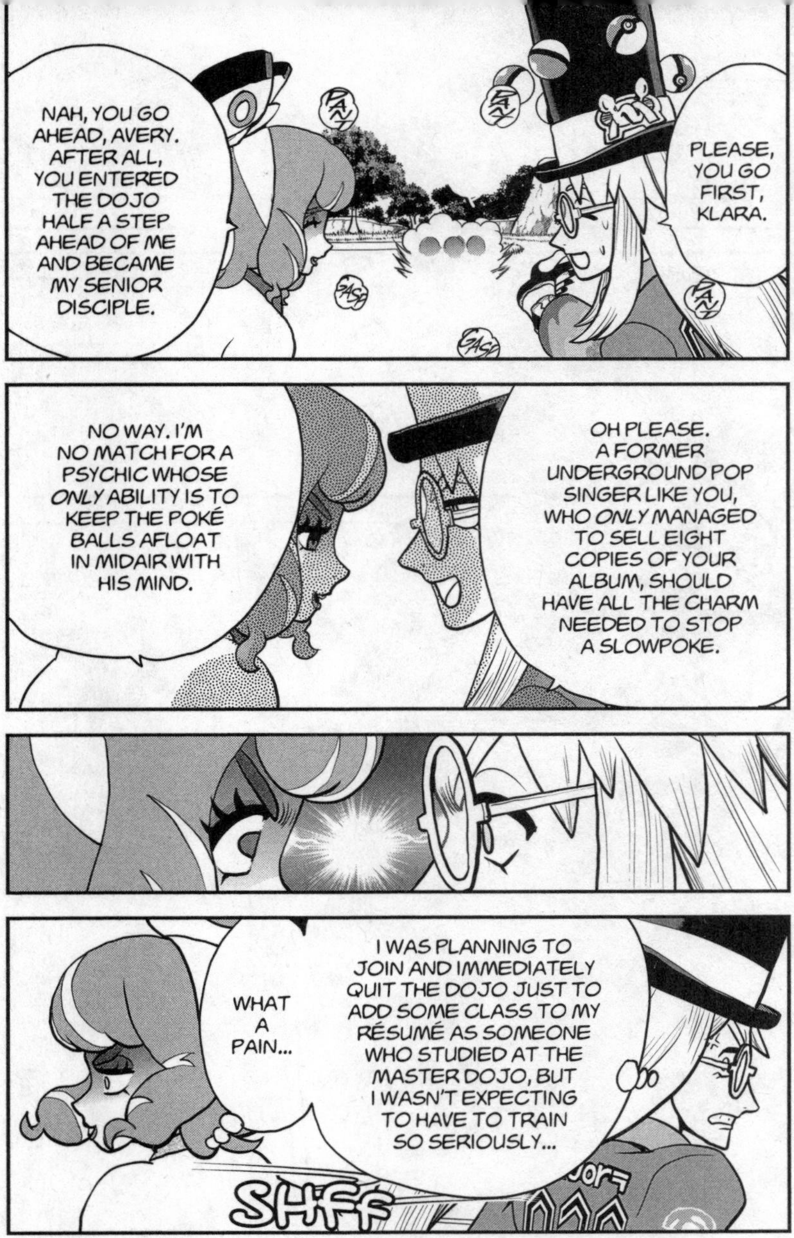
PLEASE, YOU GO FIRST, KLARA.
NAH, YOU GO AHEAD, AVERY. AFTER ALL, YOU ENTERED THE DOJO HALF A STEP AHEAD OF ME AND BECAME MY SENIOR DISCIPLE.
OH PLEASE. A FORMER UNDERGROUND POP SINGER LIKE YOU, WHO *ONLY* MANAGED TO SELL EIGHT COPIES OF YOUR ALBUM, SHOULD HAVE ALL THE CHARM NEEDED TO STOP A SLOWPOKE.
NO WAY. I'M NO MATCH FOR A PSYCHIC WHOSE *ONLY* ABILITY IS TO KEEP THE POKÉ BALLS AFLOAT IN MIDAIR WITH HIS MIND.
I WAS PLANNING TO JOIN AND IMMEDIATELY QUIT THE DOJO JUST TO ADD SOME CLASS TO MY RÉSUMÉ AS SOMEONE WHO STUDIED AT THE MASTER DOJO, BUT I WASN'T EXPECTING TO HAVE TO TRAIN SO SERIOUSLY...
WHAT A PAIN...
SHFF

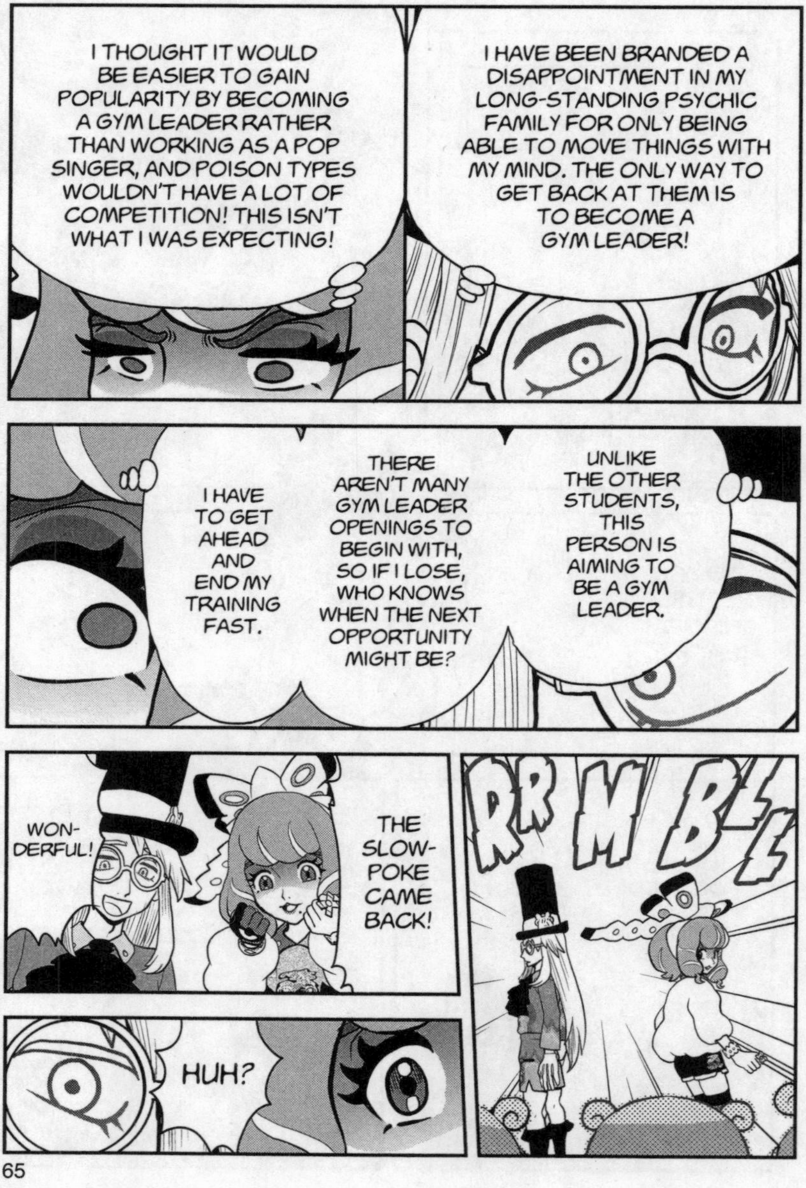
I HAVE BEEN BRANDED A DISAPPOINTMENT IN MY LONG-STANDING PSYCHIC FAMILY FOR ONLY BEING ABLE TO MOVE THINGS WITH MY MIND. THE ONLY WAY TO GET BACK AT THEM IS TO BECOME A GYM LEADER!
I THOUGHT IT WOULD BE EASIER TO GAIN POPULARITY BY BECOMING A GYM LEADER RATHER THAN WORKING AS A POP SINGER, AND POISON TYPES WOULDN'T HAVE A LOT OF COMPETITION! THIS ISN'T WHAT I WAS EXPECTING!
UNLIKE THE OTHER STUDENTS, THIS PERSON IS AIMING TO BE A GYM LEADER.
THERE AREN'T MANY GYM LEADER OPENINGS TO BEGIN WITH, SO IF I LOSE, WHO KNOWS WHEN THE NEXT OPPORTUNITY MIGHT BE?
I HAVE TO GET AHEAD AND END MY TRAINING FAST.
RR M BLE
THE SLOW-POKE CAME BACK!
WON-DERFUL!
HUH?

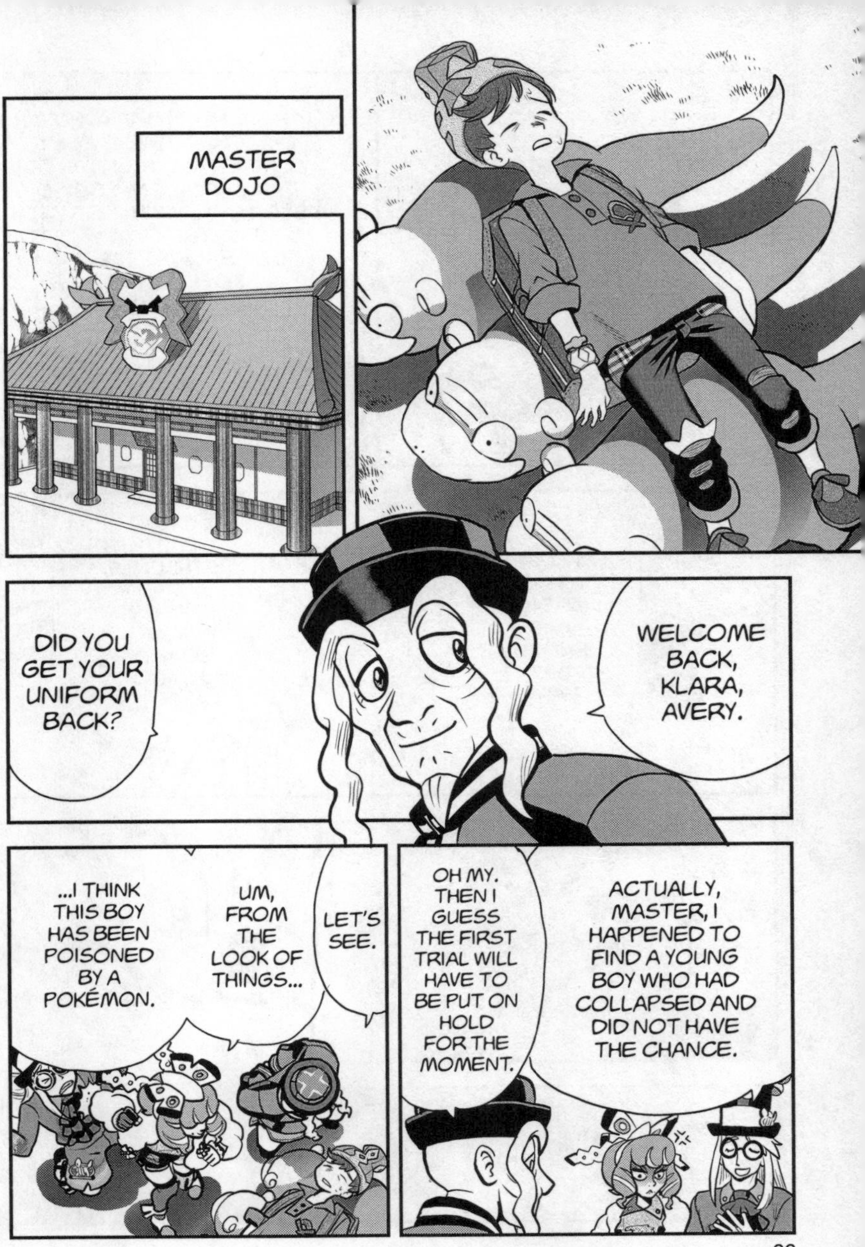
MASTER DOJO
WELCOME BACK, KLARA, AVERY.
DID YOU GET YOUR UNIFORM BACK?
ACTUALLY, MASTER, I HAPPENED TO FIND A YOUNG BOY WHO HAD COLLAPSED AND DID NOT HAVE THE CHANCE.
OH MY. THEN I GUESS THE FIRST TRIAL WILL HAVE TO BE PUT ON HOLD FOR THE MOMENT.
LET'S SEE.
UM, FROM THE LOOK OF THINGS...
...I THINK THIS BOY HAS BEEN POISONED BY A POKÉMON.

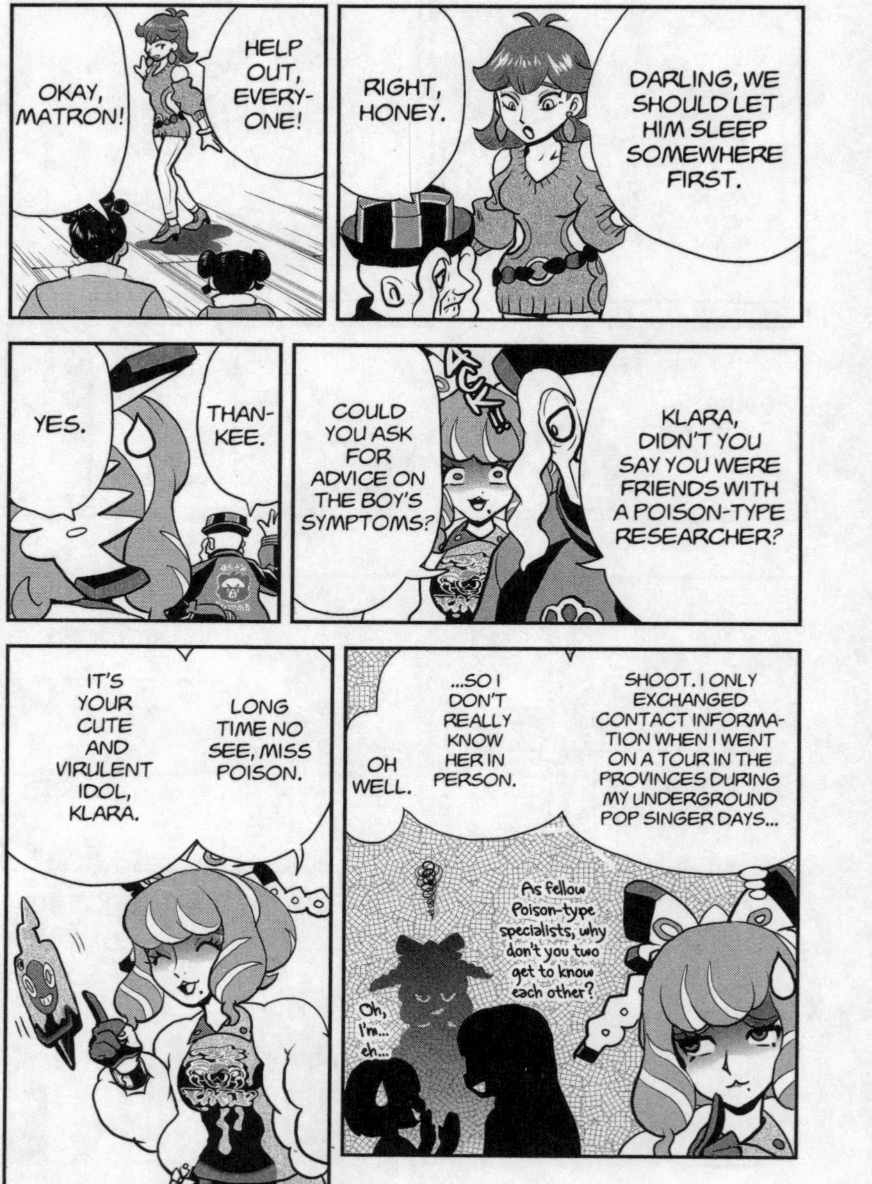
DARLING, WE SHOULD LET HIM SLEEP SOMEWHERE FIRST.
RIGHT, HONEY.
HELP OUT, EVERY-ONE!
OKAY, MATRON!
KLARA, DIDN'T YOU SAY YOU WERE FRIENDS WITH A POISON-TYPE RESEARCHER?
ACK
COULD YOU ASK FOR ADVICE ON THE BOY'S SYMPTOMS?
THAN-KEE.
YES.
SHOOT. I ONLY EXCHANGED CONTACT INFORMA-TION WHEN I WENT ON A TOUR IN THE PROVINCES DURING MY UNDERGROUND POP SINGER DAYS...
...SO I DON'T REALLY KNOW HER IN PERSON.
OH WELL.
As fellow Poison-type specialists, why don't you two get to know each other?
Oh, I'm... eh...
LONG TIME NO SEE, MISS POISON.
IT'S YOUR CUTE AND VIRULENT IDOL, KLARA.

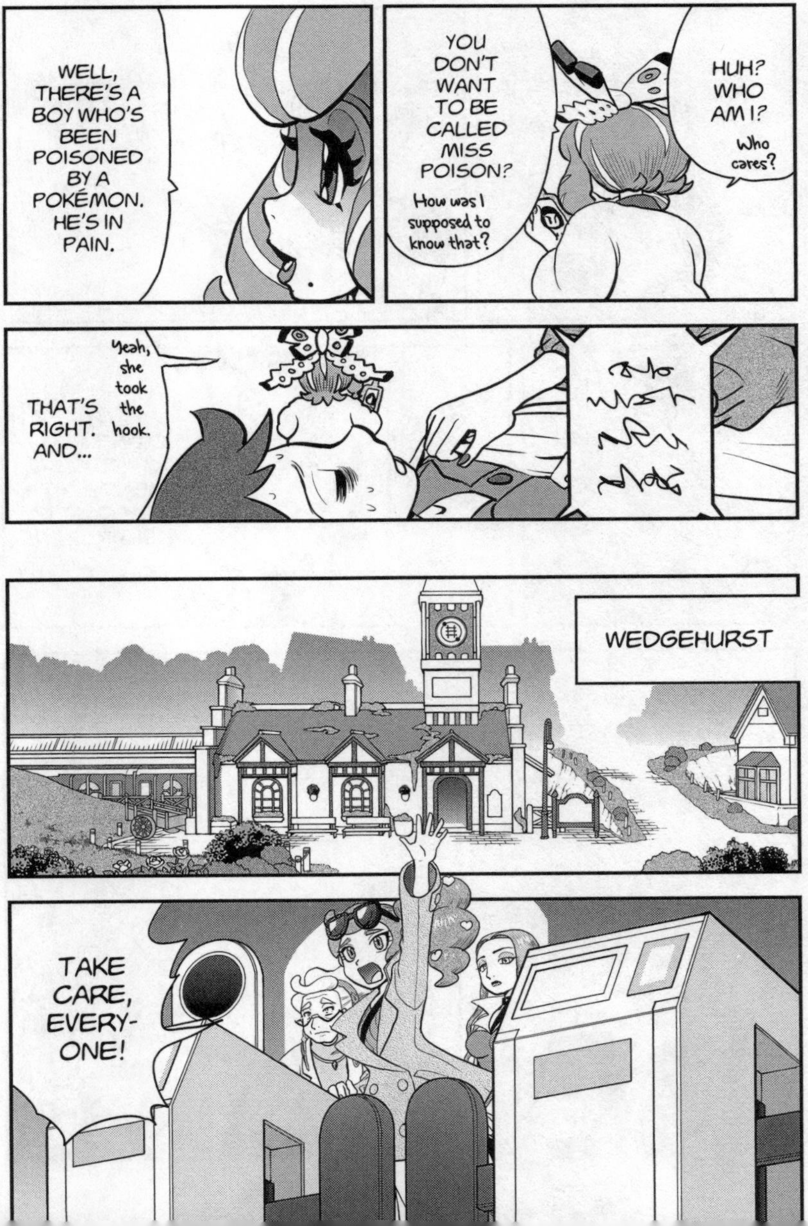
HUH? WHO AM I?
Who cares?
YOU DON'T WANT TO BE CALLED MISS POISON?
How was I supposed to know that?
WELL, THERE'S A BOY WHO'S BEEN POISONED BY A POKÉMON. HE'S IN PAIN.
Yeah, she took the hook.
THAT'S RIGHT. AND...
WEDGEHURST
TAKE CARE, EVERY-ONE!

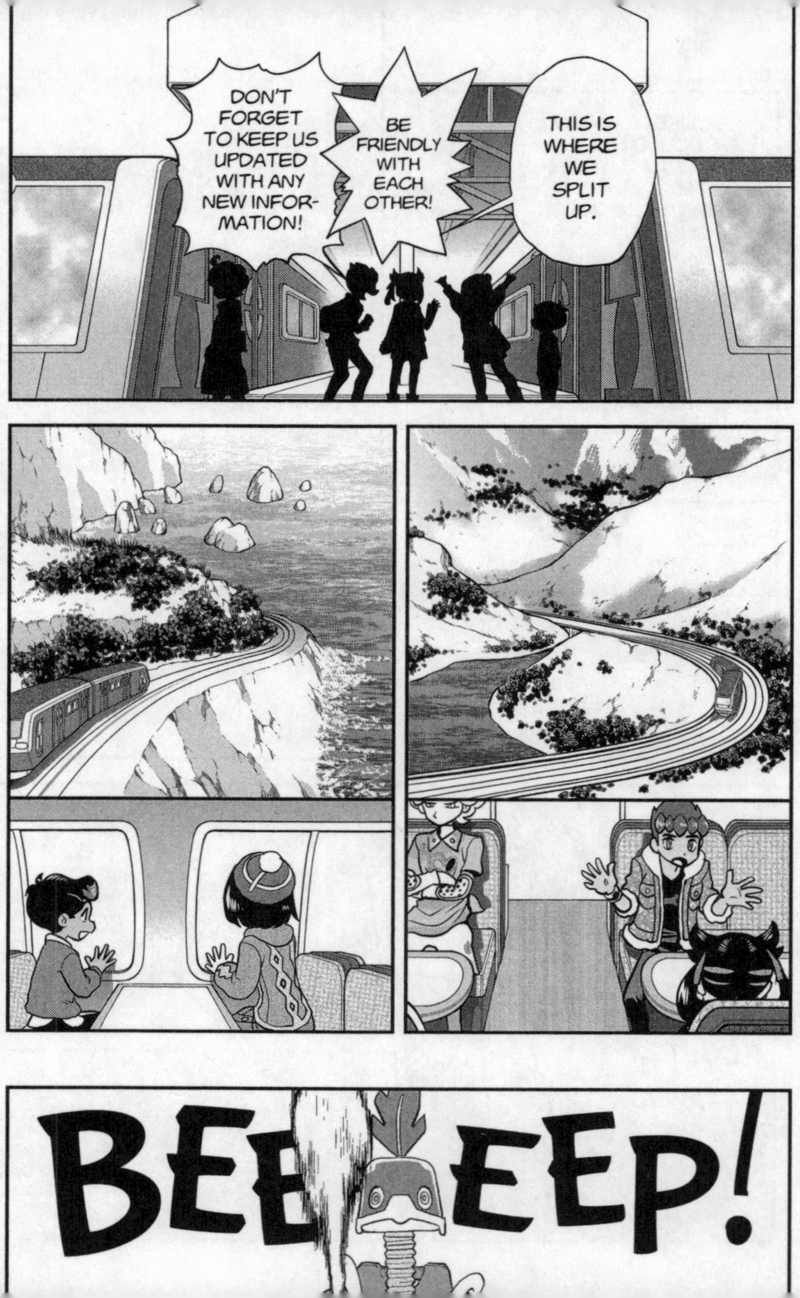
THIS IS WHERE WE SPLIT UP.
BE FRIENDLY WITH EACH OTHER!
DON'T FORGET TO KEEP US UPDATED WITH ANY NEW INFOR-MATION!
BEE EEP!

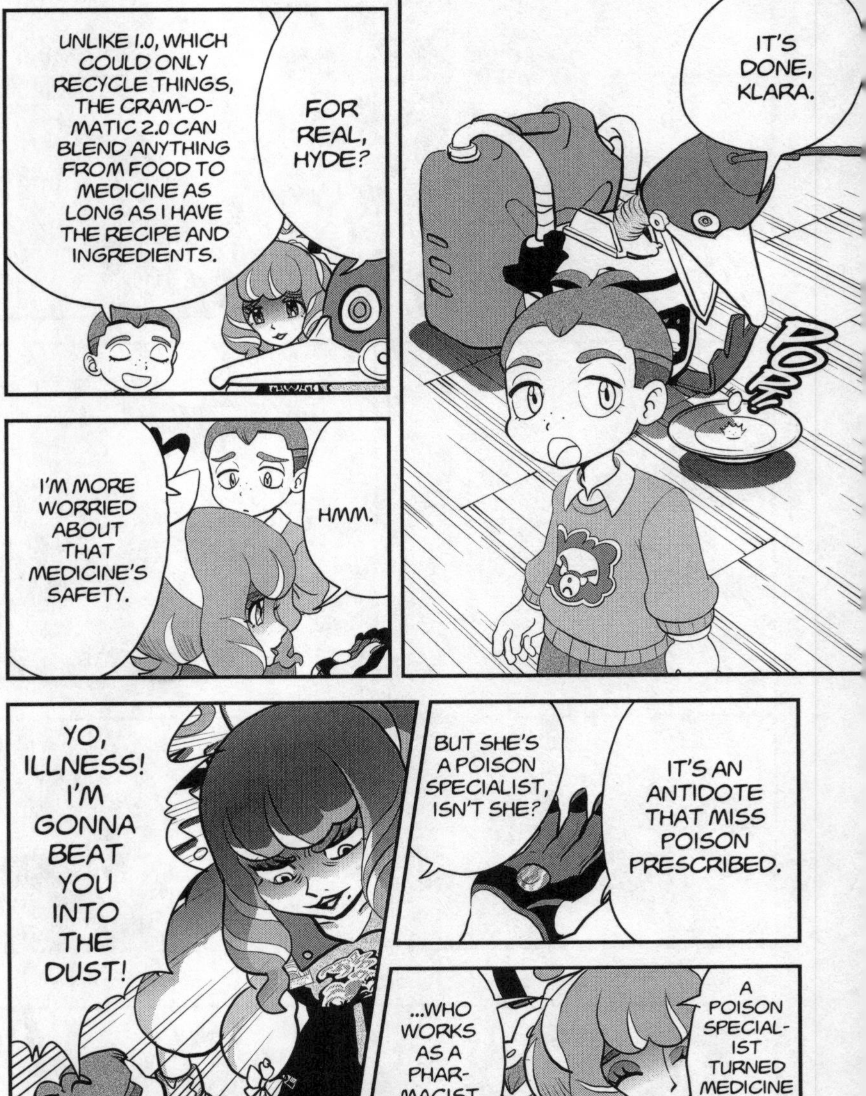
IT'S DONE, KLARA.
POP!
FOR REAL, HYDE?
UNLIKE 1.0, WHICH COULD ONLY RECYCLE THINGS, THE CRAM-O-MATIC 2.0 CAN BLEND ANYTHING FROM FOOD TO MEDICINE AS LONG AS I HAVE THE RECIPE AND INGREDIENTS.
HMM.
I'M MORE WORRIED ABOUT THAT MEDICINE'S SAFETY.
IT'S AN ANTIDOTE THAT MISS POISON PRESCRIBED.
BUT SHE'S A POISON SPECIALIST, ISN'T SHE?
A POISON SPECIAL-IST TURNED MEDICINE SPECIAL-IST...
...WHO WORKS AS A PHAR-MACIST NOW.
YO, ILLNESS! I'M GONNA BEAT YOU INTO THE DUST!

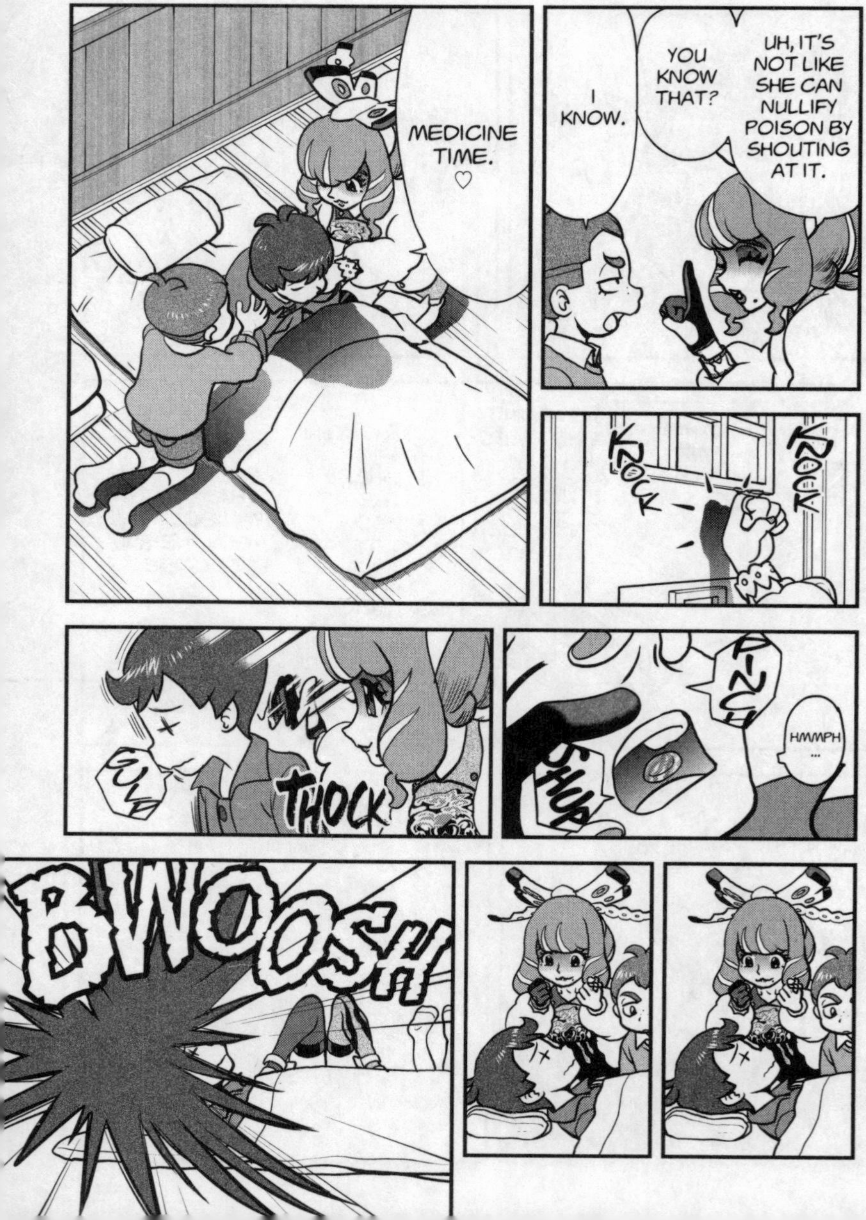
UH, IT'S NOT LIKE SHE CAN NULLIFY POISON BY SHOUTING AT IT.
YOU KNOW THAT?
I KNOW.
KNOCK
KNOCK
MEDICINE TIME. ♡
PINCH
HMMPH...
SHUP
GULP
THOCK
BWOOSH

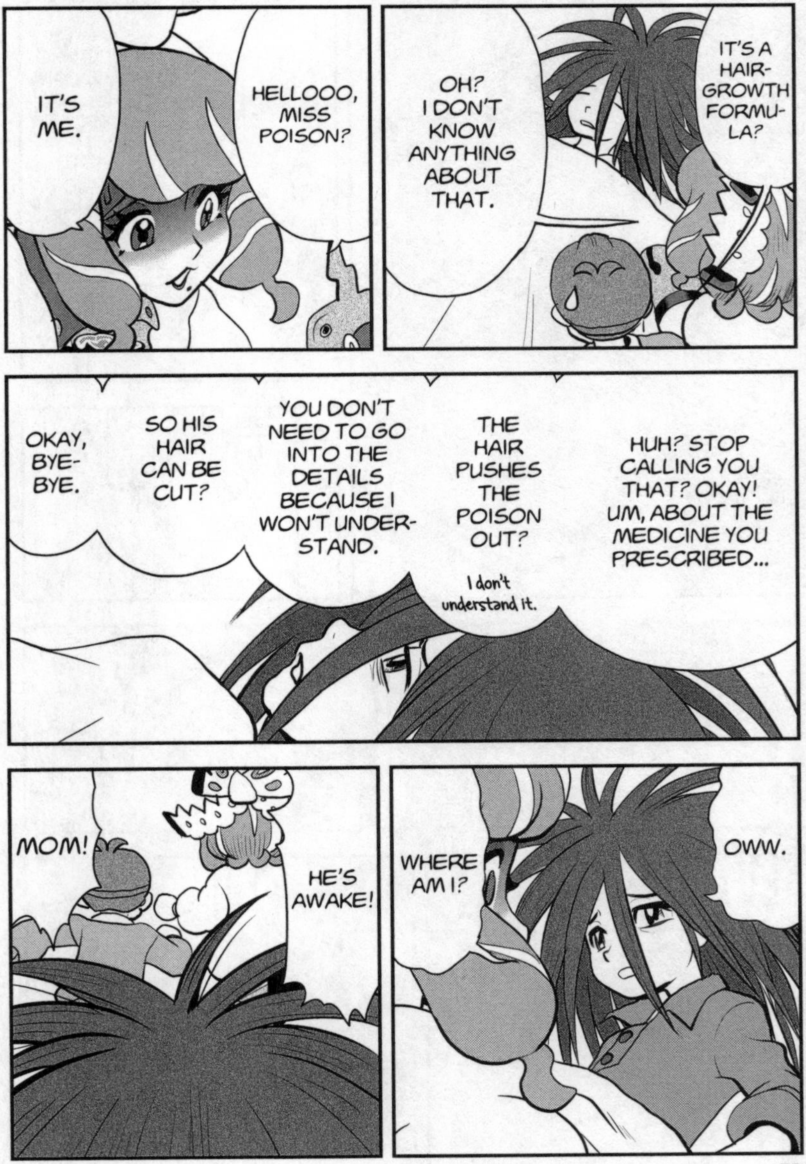
IT'S A HAIR-GROWTH FORMULA?
OH? I DON'T KNOW ANYTHING ABOUT THAT.
HELLOOO, MISS POISON?
IT'S ME.
HUH? STOP CALLING YOU THAT? OKAY! UM, ABOUT THE MEDICINE YOU PRESCRIBED...
THE HAIR PUSHES THE POISON OUT?
I don't understand it.
YOU DON'T NEED TO GO INTO THE DETAILS BECAUSE I WON'T UNDER-STAND.
SO HIS HAIR CAN BE CUT?
OKAY, BYE-BYE.
OWW.
WHERE AM I?
HE'S AWAKE!
MOM!

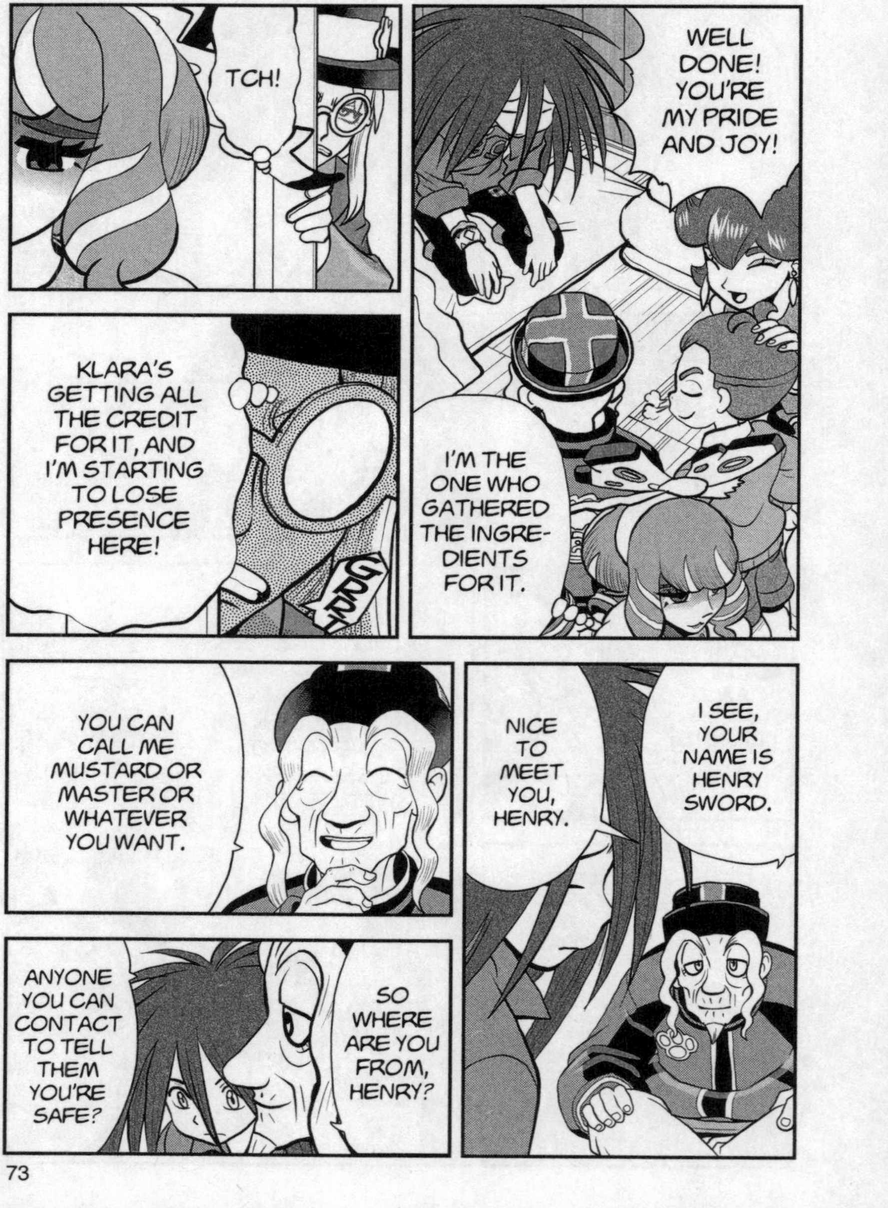
WELL DONE! YOU'RE MY PRIDE AND JOY!
I'M THE ONE WHO GATHERED THE INGRE-DIENTS FOR IT.
TCH!
KLARA'S GETTING ALL THE CREDIT FOR IT, AND I'M STARTING TO LOSE PRESENCE HERE!
I SEE, YOUR NAME IS HENRY SWORD.
NICE TO MEET YOU, HENRY.
YOU CAN CALL ME MUSTARD OR MASTER OR WHATEVER YOU WANT.
SO WHERE ARE YOU FROM, HENRY?
ANYONE YOU CAN CONTACT TO TELL THEM YOU'RE SAFE?

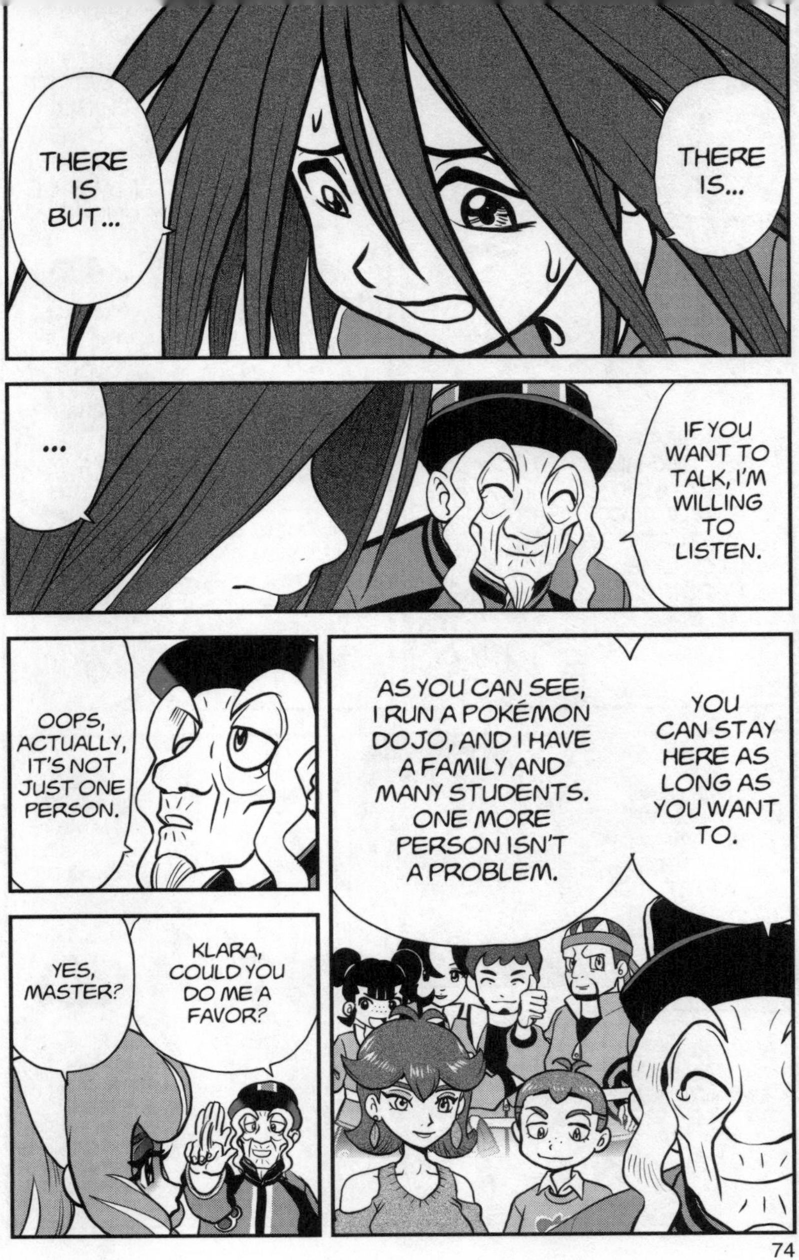
THERE IS...
THERE IS BUT...
IF YOU WANT TO TALK, I'M WILLING TO LISTEN.
...
YOU CAN STAY HERE AS LONG AS YOU WANT TO.
AS YOU CAN SEE, I RUN A POKÉMON DOJO, AND I HAVE A FAMILY AND MANY STUDENTS. ONE MORE PERSON ISN'T A PROBLEM.
OOPS, ACTUALLY, IT'S NOT JUST ONE PERSON.
KLARA, COULD YOU DO ME A FAVOR?
YES, MASTER?

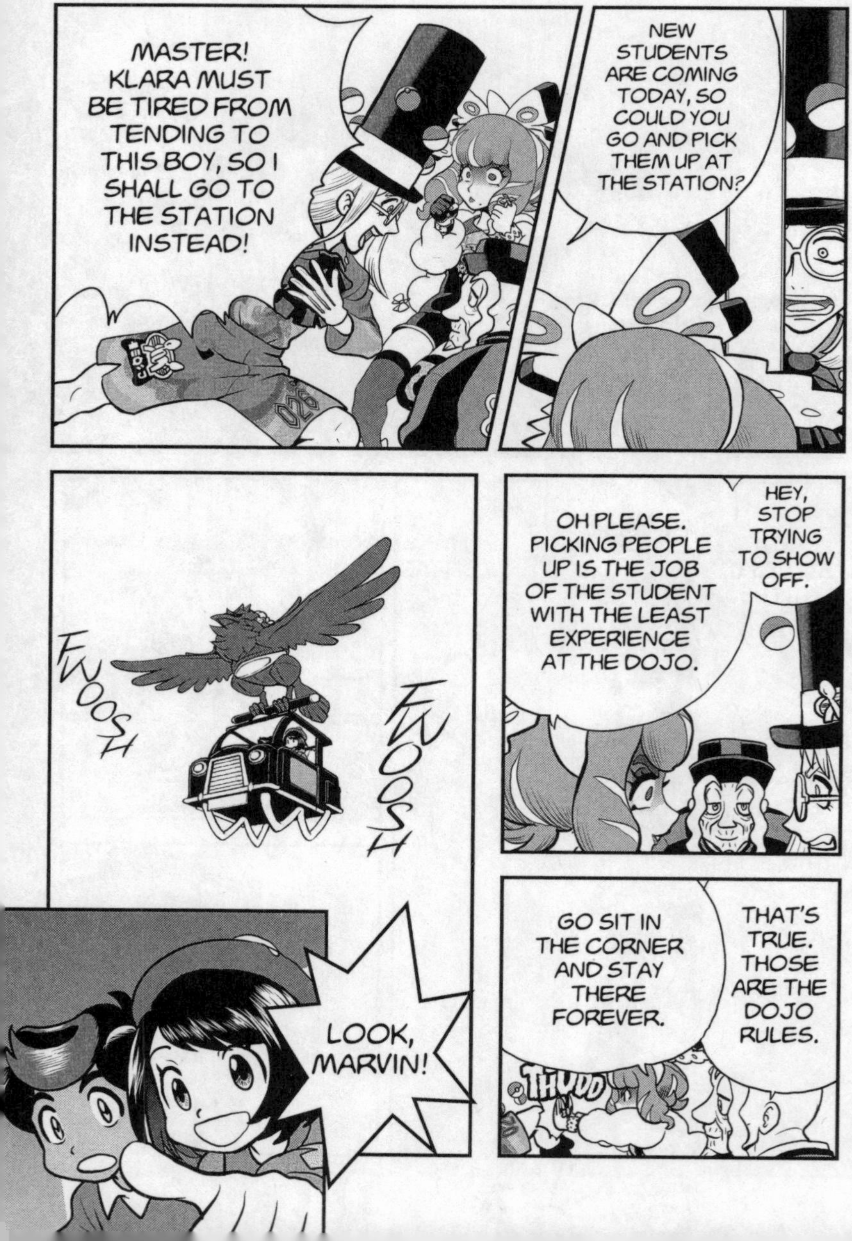
NEW STUDENTS ARE COMING TODAY, SO COULD YOU GO AND PICK THEM UP AT THE STATION?
MASTER! KLARA MUST BE TIRED FROM TENDING TO THIS BOY, SO I SHALL GO TO THE STATION INSTEAD!
HEY, STOP TRYING TO SHOW OFF.
OH PLEASE. PICKING PEOPLE UP IS THE JOB OF THE STUDENT WITH THE LEAST EXPERIENCE AT THE DOJO.
THAT'S TRUE. THOSE ARE THE DOJO RULES.
GO SIT IN THE CORNER AND STAY THERE FOREVER.
THUDD
FWOOSH
FWOOSH
LOOK, MARVIN!

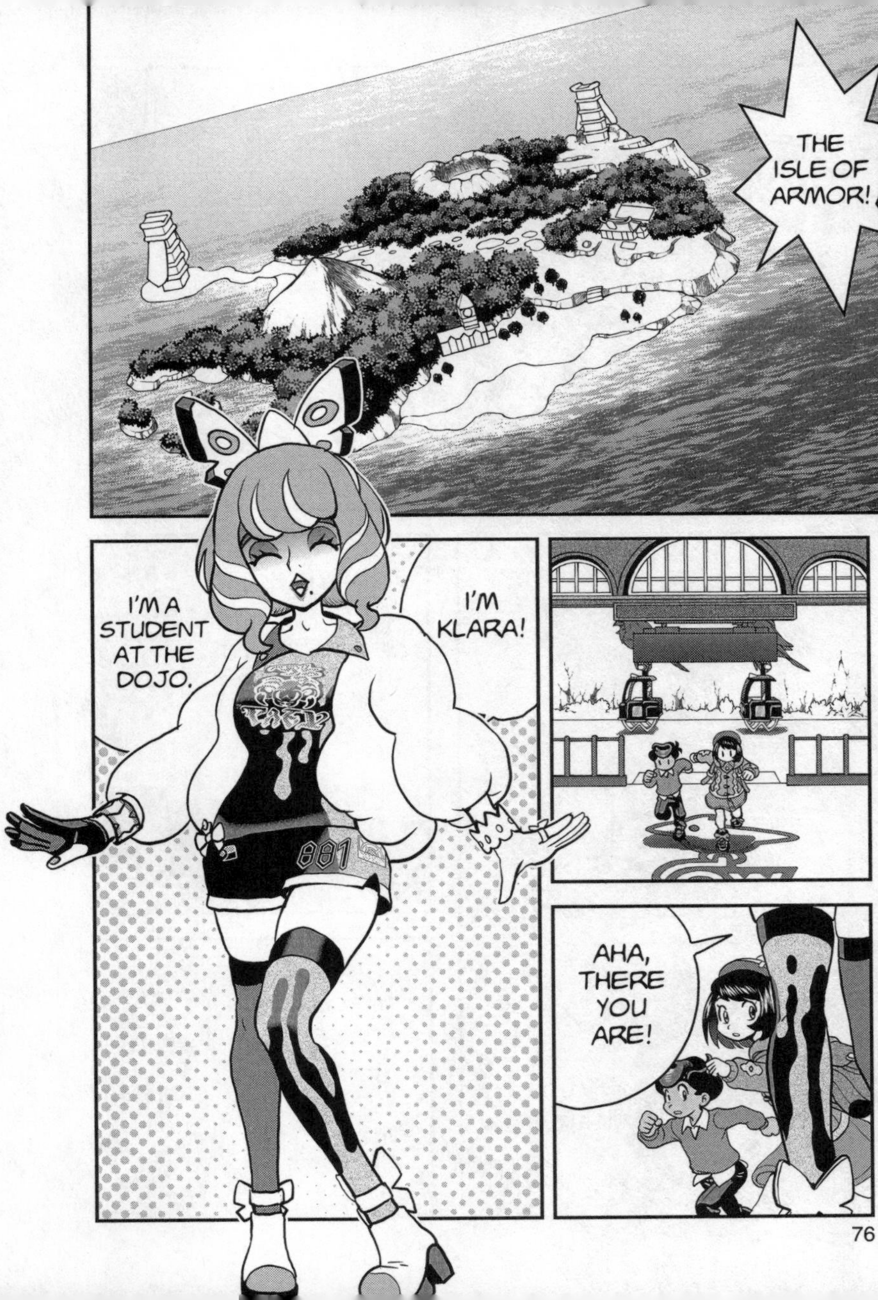
THE ISLE OF ARMOR!
AHA, THERE YOU ARE!
I'M KLARA!
I'M A STUDENT AT THE DOJO.

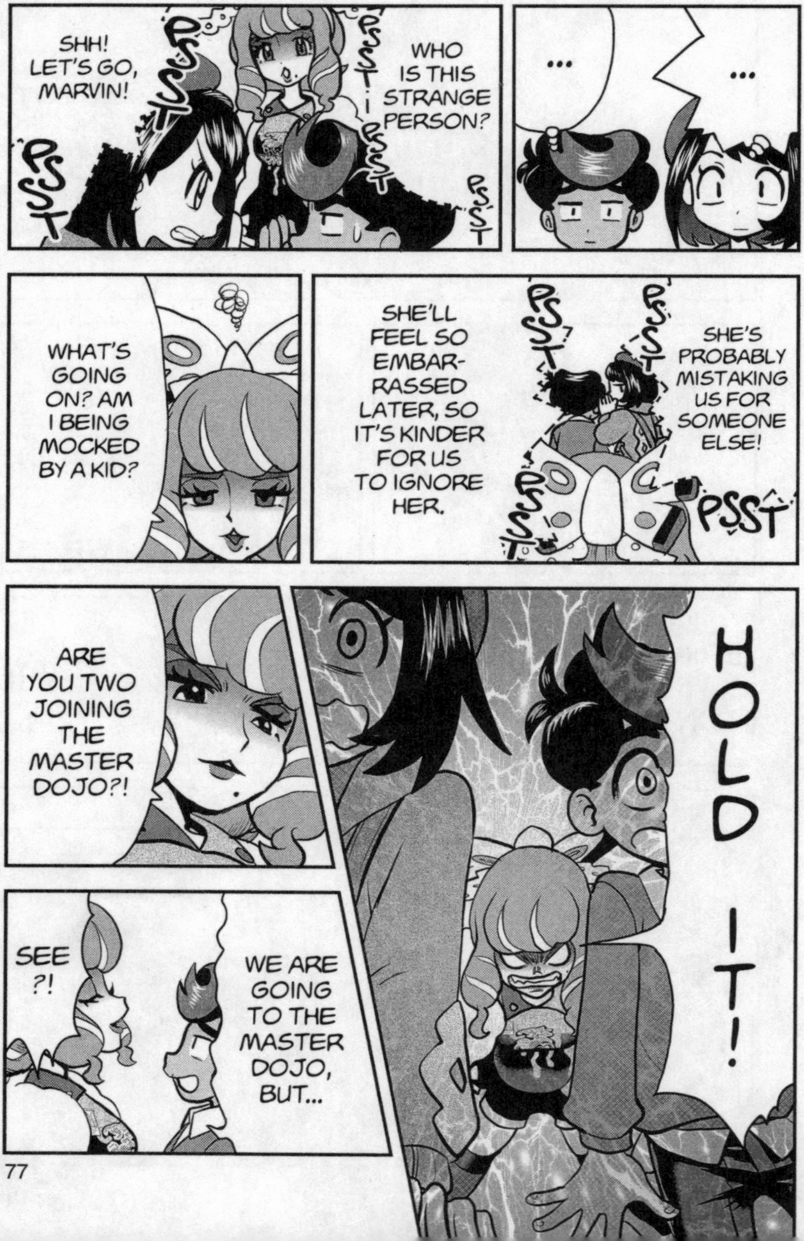
...
...
WHO IS THIS STRANGE PERSON?
SHH! LET'S GO, MARVIN!
PSST
PSST
PSST
PSST
SHE'S PROBABLY MISTAKING US FOR SOMEONE ELSE!
SHE'LL FEEL SO EMBAR-RASSED LATER, SO IT'S KINDER FOR US TO IGNORE HER.
PSST
PSST
PSST
PSST
WHAT'S GOING ON? AM I BEING MOCKED BY A KID?
HOLD IT!
ARE YOU TWO JOINING THE MASTER DOJO?!
WE ARE GOING TO THE MASTER DOJO, BUT...
SEE ?!

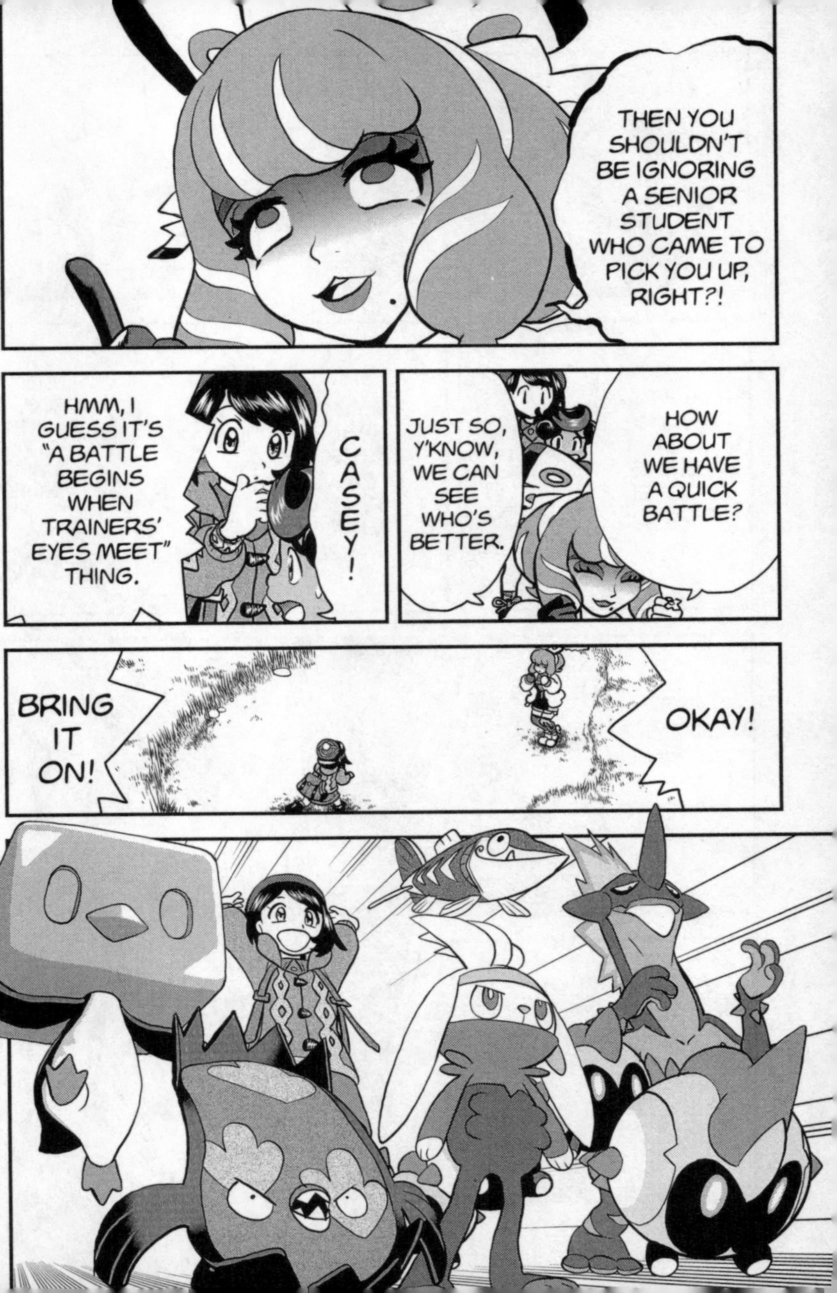
THEN YOU SHOULDN'T BE IGNORING A SENIOR STUDENT WHO CAME TO PICK YOU UP, RIGHT?!
HOW ABOUT WE HAVE A QUICK BATTLE?
JUST SO, Y'KNOW, WE CAN SEE WHO'S BETTER.
CASEY!
HMM, I GUESS IT'S "A BATTLE BEGINS WHEN TRAINERS' EYES MEET" THING.
OKAY!
BRING IT ON!

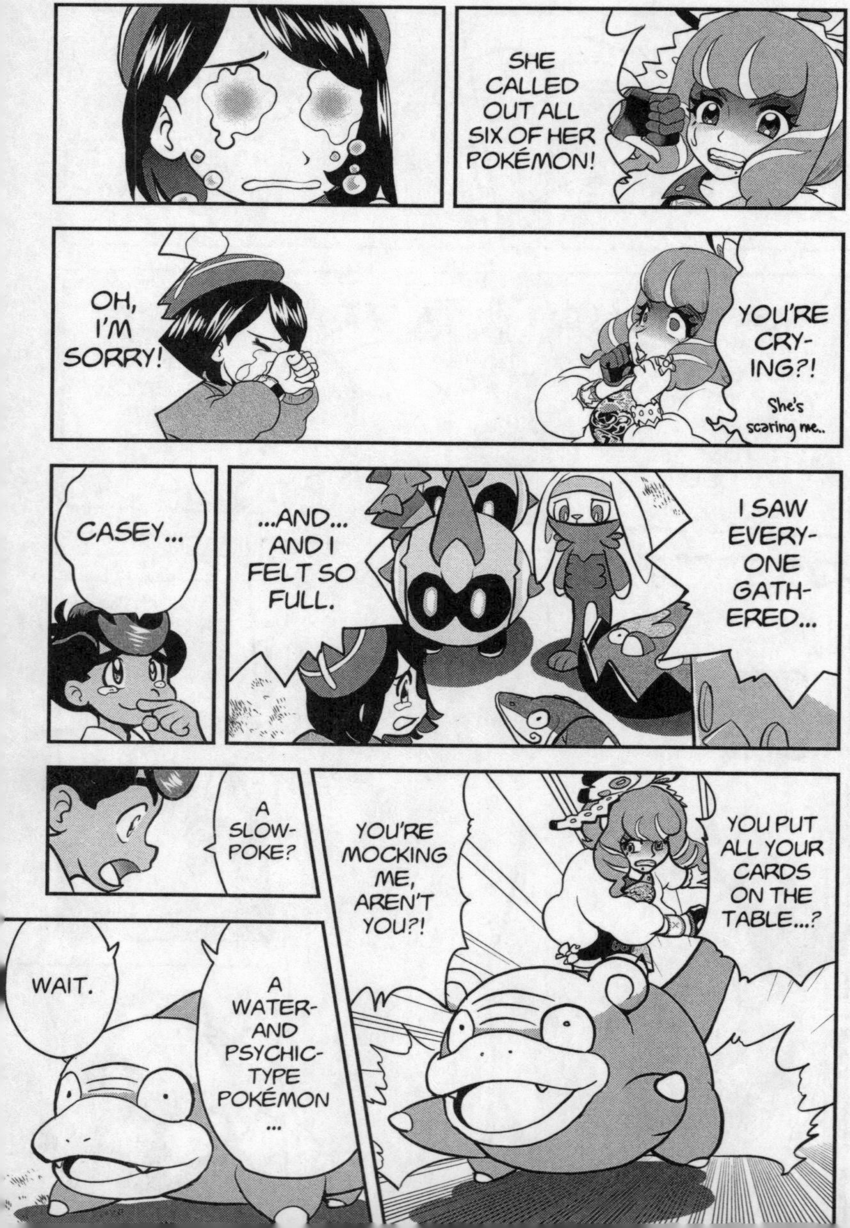
SHE CALLED OUT ALL SIX OF HER POKÉMON!
YOU'RE CRYING?!
She's scaring me..
OH, I'M SORRY!
I SAW EVERYONE GATHERED...
...AND... AND I FELT SO FULL.
CASEY...
YOU PUT ALL YOUR CARDS ON THE TABLE...?
YOU'RE MOCKING ME, AREN'T YOU?!
A SLOWPOKE?
A WATER- AND PSYCHIC-TYPE POKÉMON...
WAIT.

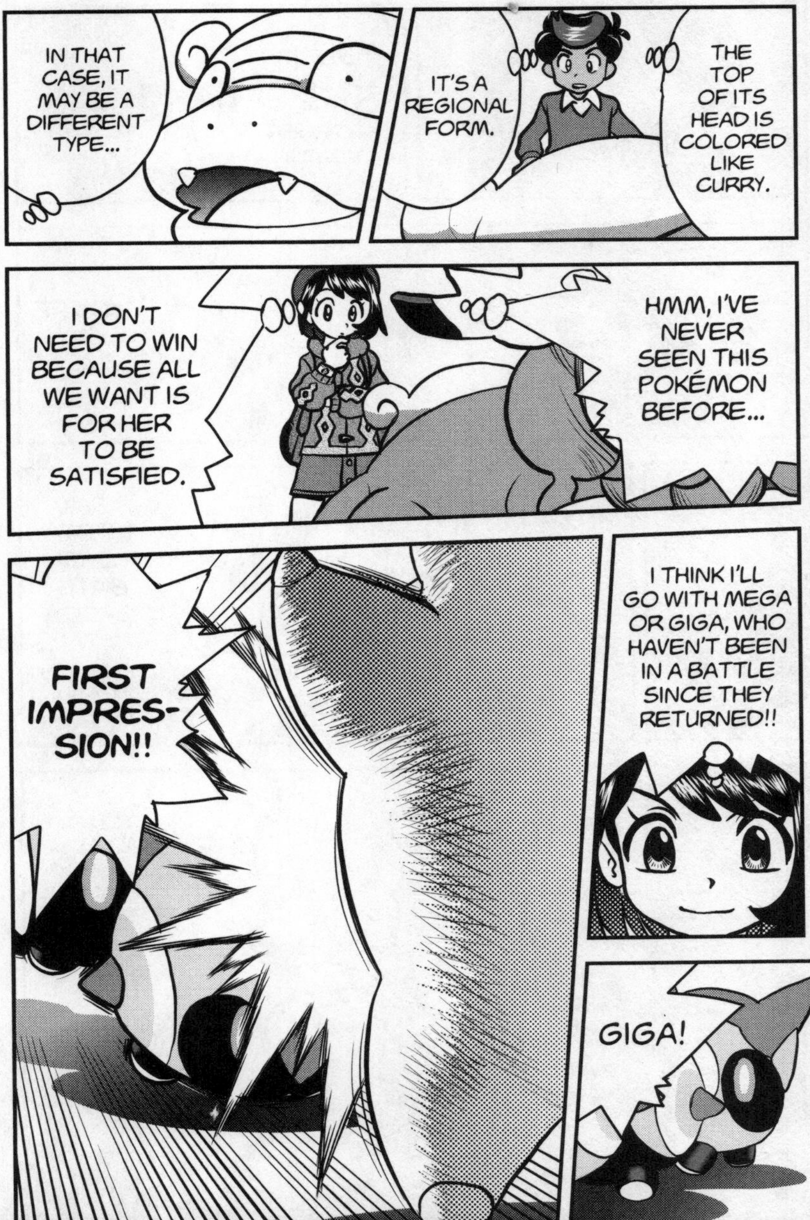
THE TOP OF ITS HEAD IS COLORED LIKE CURRY.
IT'S A REGIONAL FORM.
IN THAT CASE, IT MAY BE A DIFFERENT TYPE...
HMM, I'VE NEVER SEEN THIS POKÉMON BEFORE...
I DON'T NEED TO WIN BECAUSE ALL WE WANT IS FOR HER TO BE SATISFIED.
I THINK I'LL GO WITH MEGA OR GIGA, WHO HAVEN'T BEEN IN A BATTLE SINCE THEY RETURNED!!
GIGA!
FIRST IMPRES-SION!!

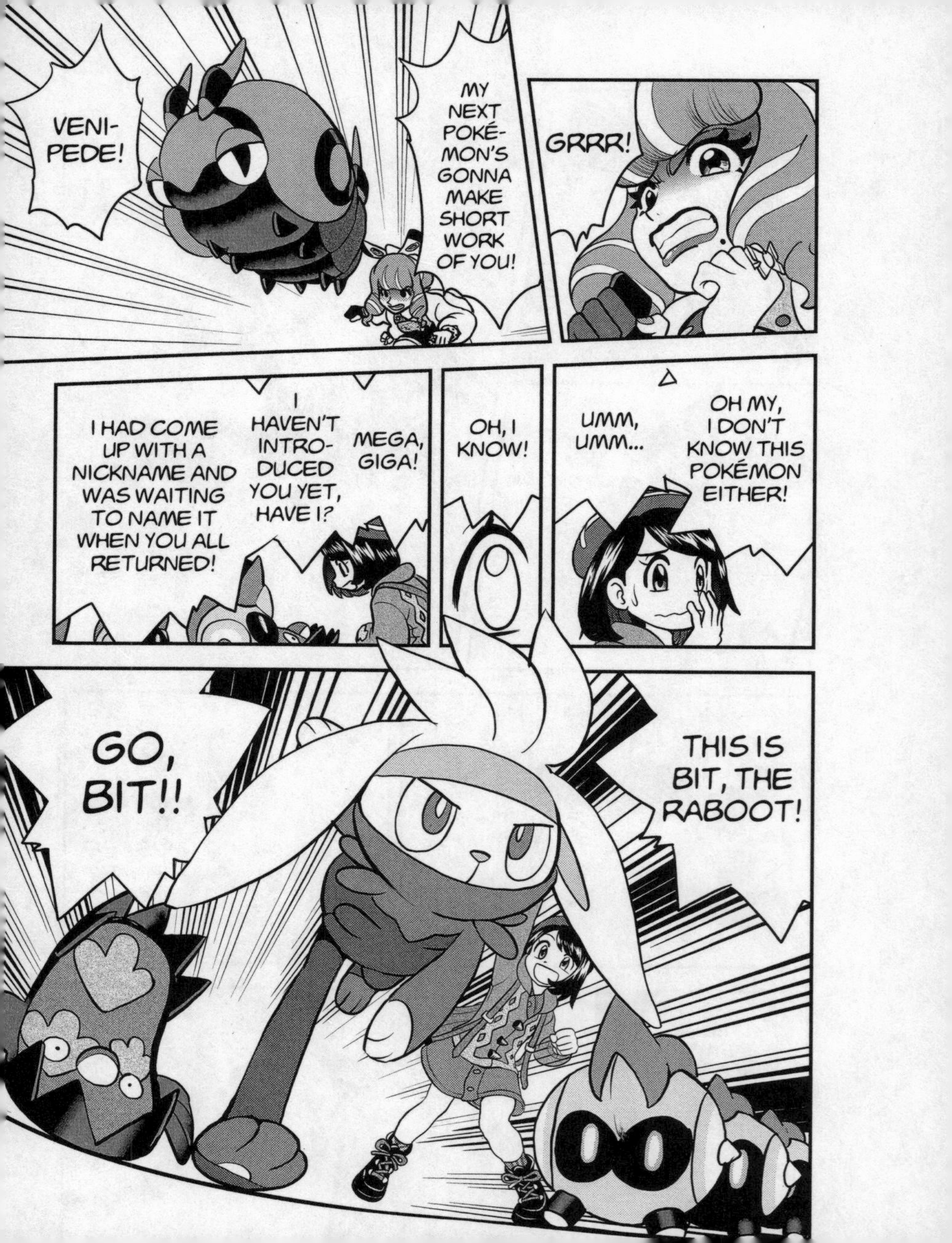
GRRR!
MY NEXT POKÉMON'S GONNA MAKE SHORT WORK OF YOU!
VENIPEDE!
OH MY, I DON'T KNOW THIS POKÉMON EITHER!
UMM, UMM...
OH, I KNOW!
MEGA, GIGA!
I HAVEN'T INTRODUCED YOU YET, HAVE I?
I HAD COME UP WITH A NICKNAME AND WAS WAITING TO NAME IT WHEN YOU ALL RETURNED!
THIS IS BIT, THE RABOOT!
GO, BIT!!

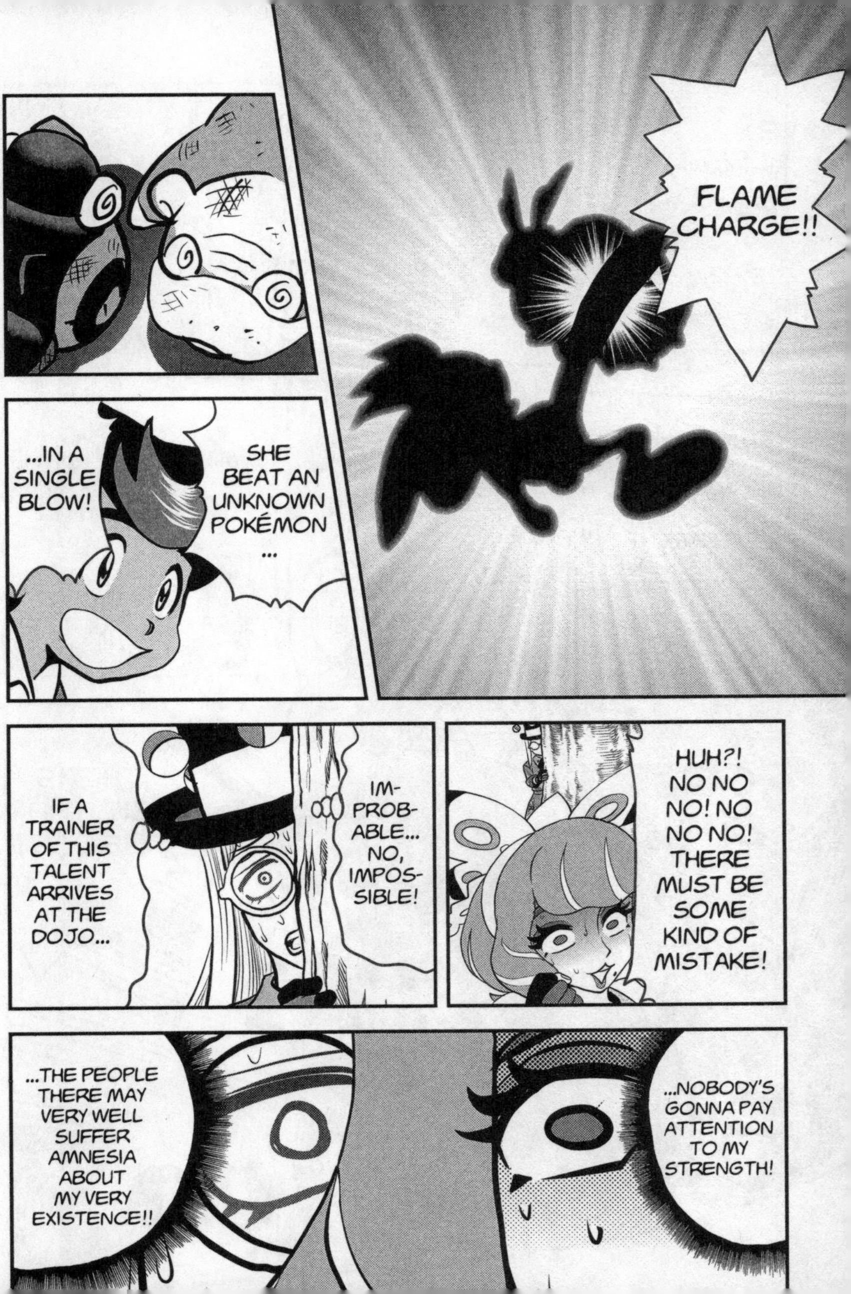
FLAME CHARGE!!
SHE BEAT AN UNKNOWN POKÉMON ...
...IN A SINGLE BLOW!
HUH?! NO NO NO! NO NO NO! THERE MUST BE SOME KIND OF MISTAKE!
IM-PROB-ABLE... NO, IMPOS-SIBLE!
IF A TRAINER OF THIS TALENT ARRIVES AT THE DOJO...
...NOBODY'S GONNA PAY ATTENTION TO MY STRENGTH!
...THE PEOPLE THERE MAY VERY WELL SUFFER AMNESIA ABOUT MY VERY EXISTENCE!!

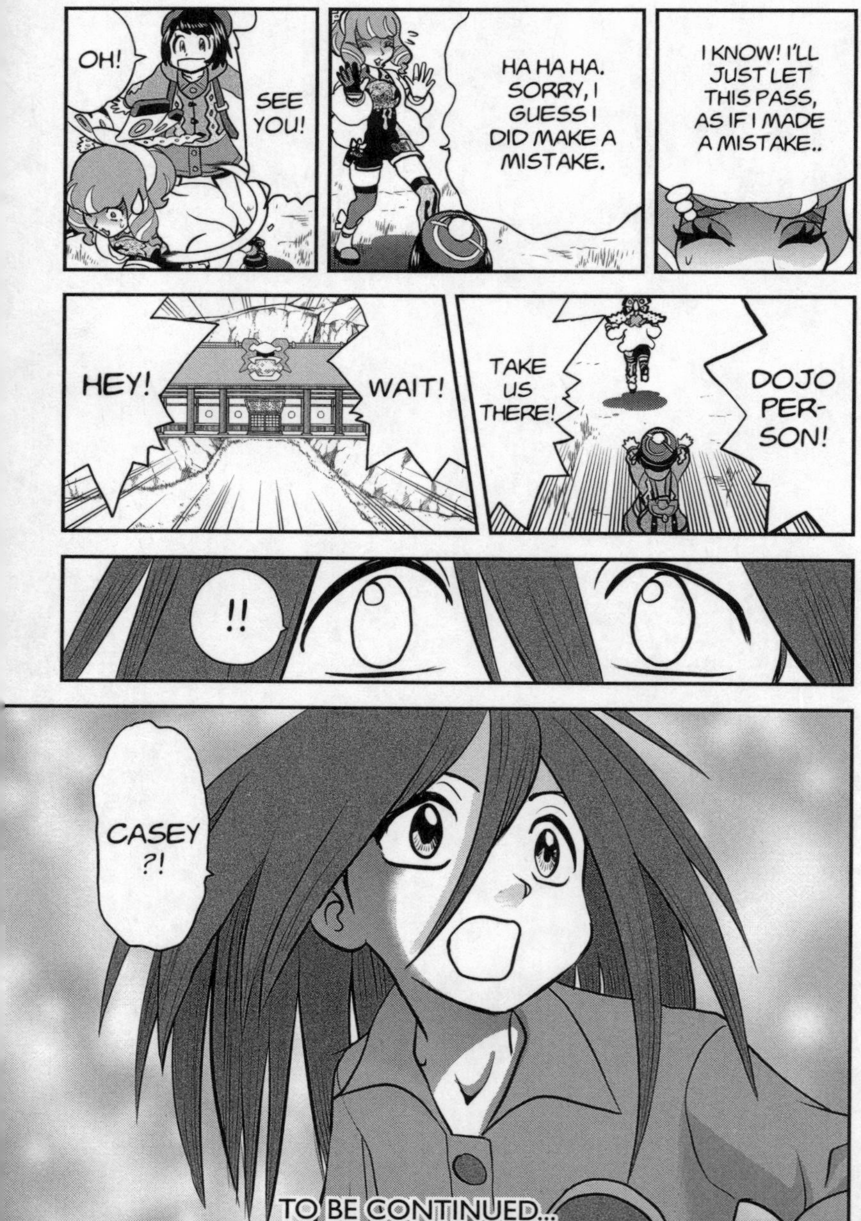
I KNOW! I'LL JUST LET THIS PASS, AS IF I MADE A MISTAKE..
HA HA HA. SORRY, I GUESS I DID MAKE A MISTAKE.
OH!
SEE YOU!
DOJO PER-SON!
TAKE US THERE!
WAIT!
HEY!
!!
CASEY ?!
TO BE CONTINUED...

POKÉMON™
SWORD & SHIELD

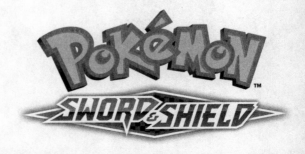

HENRY SWORD – POKÉMON DATA

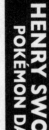

KAYNE LV. 42

(MR. RIME ♂)

GEAR: Cane

THE FIFTH AND MOST RECENT ADDITION TO THE TEAM. A TRUE ENTERTAINER WHO AMUSES PEOPLE WITH ITS TAP DANCING AND FUNNY MOVES.

CATEGORY	Comedian Pokémon	**ABILITY**	Screen Cleaner
TYPE	Ice/Psychic	**EGG**	Discovered
HEIGHT	4'11"	Galar Pokédex Number	**366**
WEIGHT	128.3 lbs		

FANGURU LV. 35

(ORANGURU ♂)

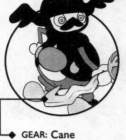

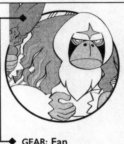

GEAR: Fan

AS A SAGE POKÉMON, IT IS HIGHLY INTELLIGENT. FANGURU'S PRESENCE WILL DEFINITELY BE NEEDED IN A BATTLE OF WITS IN THE FUTURE!!

CATEGORY	Sage Pokémon	**ABILITY**	Telepathy
TYPE	Normal/Psychic	**EGG**	Discovered
HEIGHT	4'11"	Galar Pokédex Number	**342**
WEIGHT	167.6 lbs		

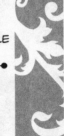

STEELER LV. 32

(GURDURR ♂)

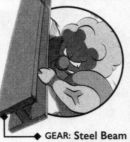

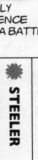

GEAR: Steel Beam

STEELER IS A POWERFUL POKÉMON WHO WILL DEFINITELY HAVE THE ADVANTAGE IN A BATTLE OF SHEER STRENGTH. HENRY HAS HEATED AND FORGED ITS GEAR, WHICH HAS BECOME MUCH HARDER THAN BEFORE.

CATEGORY	Muscular Pokémon	**ABILITY**	Guts
TYPE	Fighting	**EGG**	Discovered
HEIGHT	3'11"	Galar Pokédex Number	**172**
WEIGHT	88.2 lbs		

LANCELOT LV. 36

(SIRFETCH'D ♂)

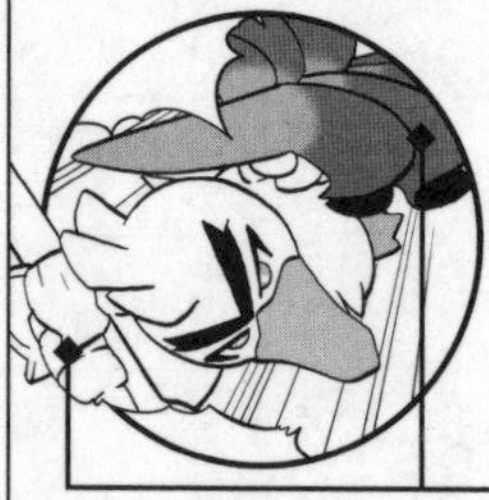

GEAR: Leek, Leek Leaf

LANCELOT IS THE OLDEST MEMBER OF THE TEAM AND INSPIRES THE OTHERS. HOW WILL IT FIGHT IN THE UPCOMING REMATCH AGAINST ETERNATUS?

CATEGORY	Wild Duck Pokémon	ABILITY	Steadfast
TYPE	Fighting	EGG	Discovered
HEIGHT	2'07"	Galar Pokédex Number	219
WEIGHT	257.9 lbs		

TWIGGY LV. 34

(THWACKEY ♂)

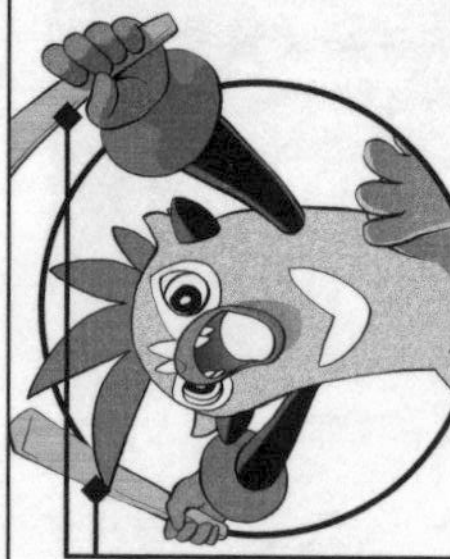

GEAR: Stick

TWIGGY IS EXPECTED TO MAKE EVEN MORE PROGRESS WITH ADDITIONAL TRAINING. WE CAN'T WAIT TO SEE IT GROW STRONGER ON THE ISLE OF ARMOR!!

CATEGORY	Beat Pokémon	ABILITY	Overgrow
TYPE	Grass	EGG	Discovered
HEIGHT	2'04"	Galar Pokédex Number	002
WEIGHT	30.9 lbs		

WHAT IS THE "SECRET ARMOR"?!

A TALE THAT HAS BEEN PASSED DOWN FOR GENERATIONS ON THE ISLE OF ARMOR. WHAT COULD IT BE? IF IT'S POKÉMON GEAR, HOW WILL HENRY REACT TO IT? WE MUST STAY FOCUSED!!

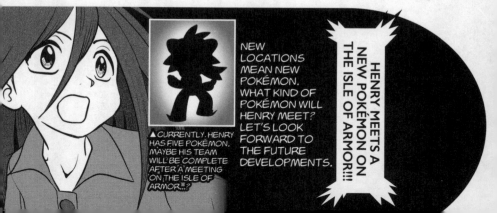

HENRY MEETS A NEW POKÉMON ON THE ISLE OF ARMOR!!!

NEW LOCATIONS MEAN NEW POKÉMON. WHAT KIND OF POKÉMON WILL HENRY MEET? LET'S LOOK FORWARD TO THE FUTURE DEVELOPMENTS.

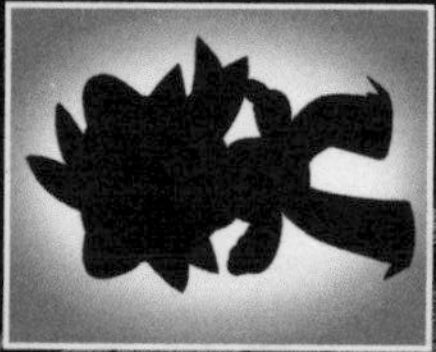

▲CURRENTLY, HENRY HAS FIVE POKÉMON. MAYBE HIS TEAM WILL BE COMPLETE AFTER A MEETING ON THE ISLE OF ARMOR...?

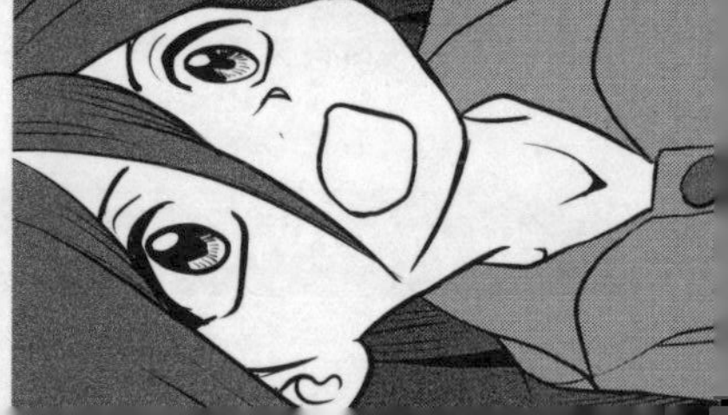

ISLE OF ARMOR

LAND!!!

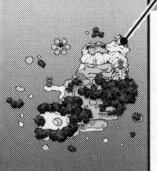

THE GALAR REGION HAS BEEN THROWN INTO CHAOS BECAUSE OF THE DARKEST DAY. IN ORDER TO FACE ETERNATUS, WE MUST FIND THE "RUSTED SWORD" AND "RUSTED SHIELD" FOR ZACIAN AND ZAMAZENTA. IT'S SAID THE ISLE OF ARMOR IS WHERE THEY CAN BE FOUND!

THE ARMOR PASS YOU NEED TO GO TO THE ISLE OF ARMOR, THE SOLITARY ISLAND...
...AND THE CROWN PASS YOU NEED TO ENTER THE CROWN TUNDRA.
I'VE PRE-PARED FIVE OF EACH.

▲ OLEANA, CHAIRMAN ROSE'S SECRETARY, PREPARED THE PASSES. THE PATH TO A NEW LOCATION HAS OPENED UP FOR THE FIVE TRAINERS!

A SOLITARY ISLAND

THE ISLE OF ARMOR IS LOCATED AWAY FROM THE MAINLAND. IT IS SUR-ROUNDED BY THE SEA AND IS NOT AN EASY PLACE TO GET TO.

A FAMOUS TRAINING GROUND

THE MASTER DOJO RUN BY MUSTARD IS LOCATED ON THE ISLAND. LEON IS SAID TO HAVE TRAINED THERE TOO...?!

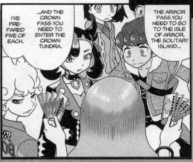

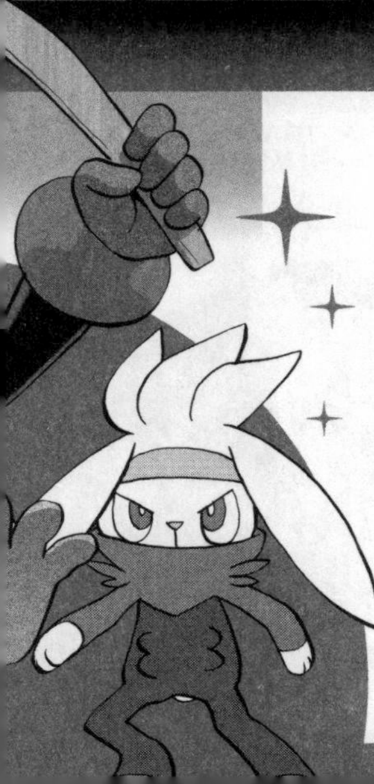

NEW GIGANTAMAXING?!

POKÉMON WHO WERE BELIEVED TO ONLY DYNAMAX HAVE A NEW FORM? WHAT COULD IT MEAN?

CROWN TUNDRA

ANOTHER LOCATION THAT CASEY POINTED OUT IS THE CROWN TUNDRA. IT IS A DIFFERENT LOCATION FAR AWAY FROM THE ISLE OF ARMOR, BUT WHAT WILL HAPPEN THERE?! THE YOUNG TRAINERS, MARVIN, HOP, BEDE, AND MARNIE HAVE GONE THERE. AND A NEW STORY OF TRAINING AND ADVENTURE IS ABOUT TO UNFOLD.

TO THE NEW

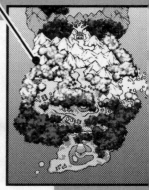

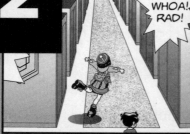

WHOA! RAD!

▲ CASEY THE COMPUTER TECHNICIAN IS OVERJOYED. IT IS THANKS TO THIS FACILITY THAT SHE WAS ABLE TO FIND OUT WHERE THE GEARS HAD GONE!

A SNOW-CLAD AREA

THE CROWN TUNDRA IS LOCATED ON THE GALAR MAINLAND, BUT NOT MANY PEOPLE HAVE SET FOOT THERE.

HAMPERED BY HEAVY SNOW

THE GREATEST ENEMY HERE IS "SNOW." WEARING COLD PROTECTION ON YOUR ADVENTURE IS A MUST!

RUMORS OF A LEGEND?!

BIRDS FLY ACROSS THE SNOWY TUNDRA; MYSTERIOUS BRAILLE AND POKÉMON—THE CROWN TUNDRA IS FILLED WITH ALL SORTS OF INTEREST-ING LEGENDS.

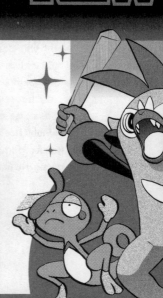

Hidenori Kusaka is the writer for *Pokémon Adventures*. Running continuously for over 25 years, *Pokémon Adventures* is the only manga series to completely cover all the *Pokémon* games and has become one of the most popular series of all time. In addition to writing manga, he also edits children's books and plans mixed-media projects for Shogakukan's children's magazines. He uses the Pokémon Electrode as his author portrait.

———————————

Satoshi Yamamoto is the artist for *Pokémon Adventures*, which he began working on in 2001, starting with volume 10. Yamamoto launched his manga career in 1993 with the horror-action title *Kimen Senshi*, which ran in Shogakukan's *Weekly Shonen Sunday* magazine, followed by the series *Kaze no Denshosha*. Yamamoto's favorite manga creators/artists include FUJIKO F FUJIO (*Doraemon*), Yukinobu Hoshino (*2001 Nights*), and Katsuhiro Otomo (*Akira*). He loves films, monsters, detective novels, and punk rock music. He uses the Pokémon Swalot as his artist portrait.

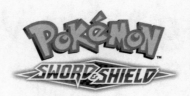

**Pokémon: Sword & Shield
Volume 10
VIZ Media Edition**

Story by HIDENORI KUSAKA
Art by SATOSHI YAMAMOTO

©2024 Pokémon.
©1995–2022 Nintendo / Creatures Inc. / GAME FREAK inc.
TM, ®, and character names are trademarks of Nintendo.
© 2020 Hidenori KUSAKA, Satoshi YAMAMOTO
All rights reserved.
Original Japanese edition published by SHOGAKUKAN.
English translation rights in the United States of America, Canada, the United Kingdom,
Ireland, Australia and New Zealand arranged with SHOGAKUKAN.

Original Cover Design—Hiroyuki KAWASOME (grafio)

Translation—Tetsuichiro Miyaki
English Adaptation—Molly Tanzer
Touch-Up & Lettering—Annaliese "Ace" Christman
Cover Color—Philana Chen
Design—Alice Lewis
Editor—Joel Enos

Special thanks to Trish Ledoux and Wendy Hoover at The Pokémon Company International.

Printed in the U.S.A.

Published by VIZ Media, LLC
P.O. Box 77010
San Francisco, CA 94107

10 9 8 7 6 5 4 3 2 1
First printing, August 2024

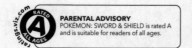

PARENTAL ADVISORY
POKÉMON: SWORD & SHIELD is rated A
and is suitable for readers of all ages.

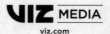

viz.com

Coming Next Volume

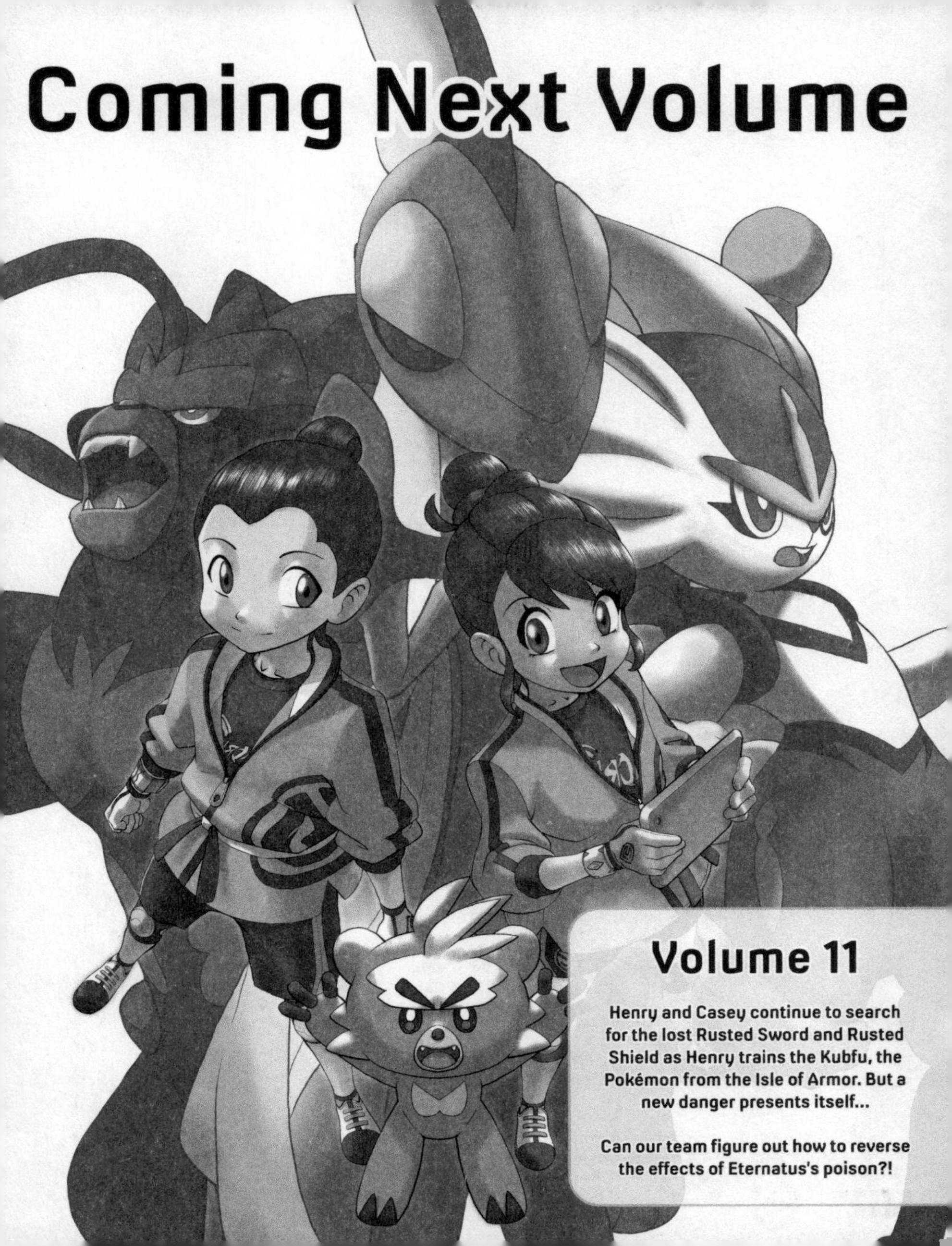

Volume 11

Henry and Casey continue to search for the lost Rusted Sword and Rusted Shield as Henry trains the Kubfu, the Pokémon from the Isle of Armor. But a new danger presents itself...

Can our team figure out how to reverse the effects of Eternatus's poison?!

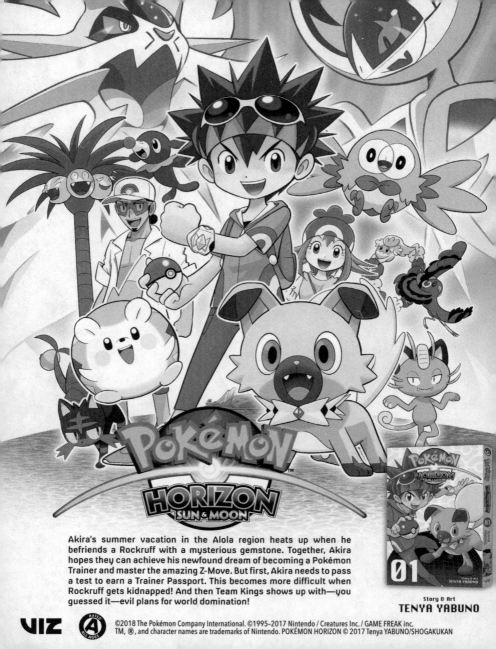

Pokémon

HORIZON IN SUN & MOON

Akira's summer vacation in the Alola region heats up when he befriends a Rockruff with a mysterious gemstone. Together, Akira hopes they can achieve his newfound dream of becoming a Pokémon Trainer and master the amazing Z-Move. But first, Akira needs to pass a test to earn a Trainer Passport. This becomes more difficult when Rockruff gets kidnapped! And then Team Kings shows up with—you guessed it—evil plans for world domination!

Story & Art
TENYA YABUNO

VIZ

RATED A ALL AGES

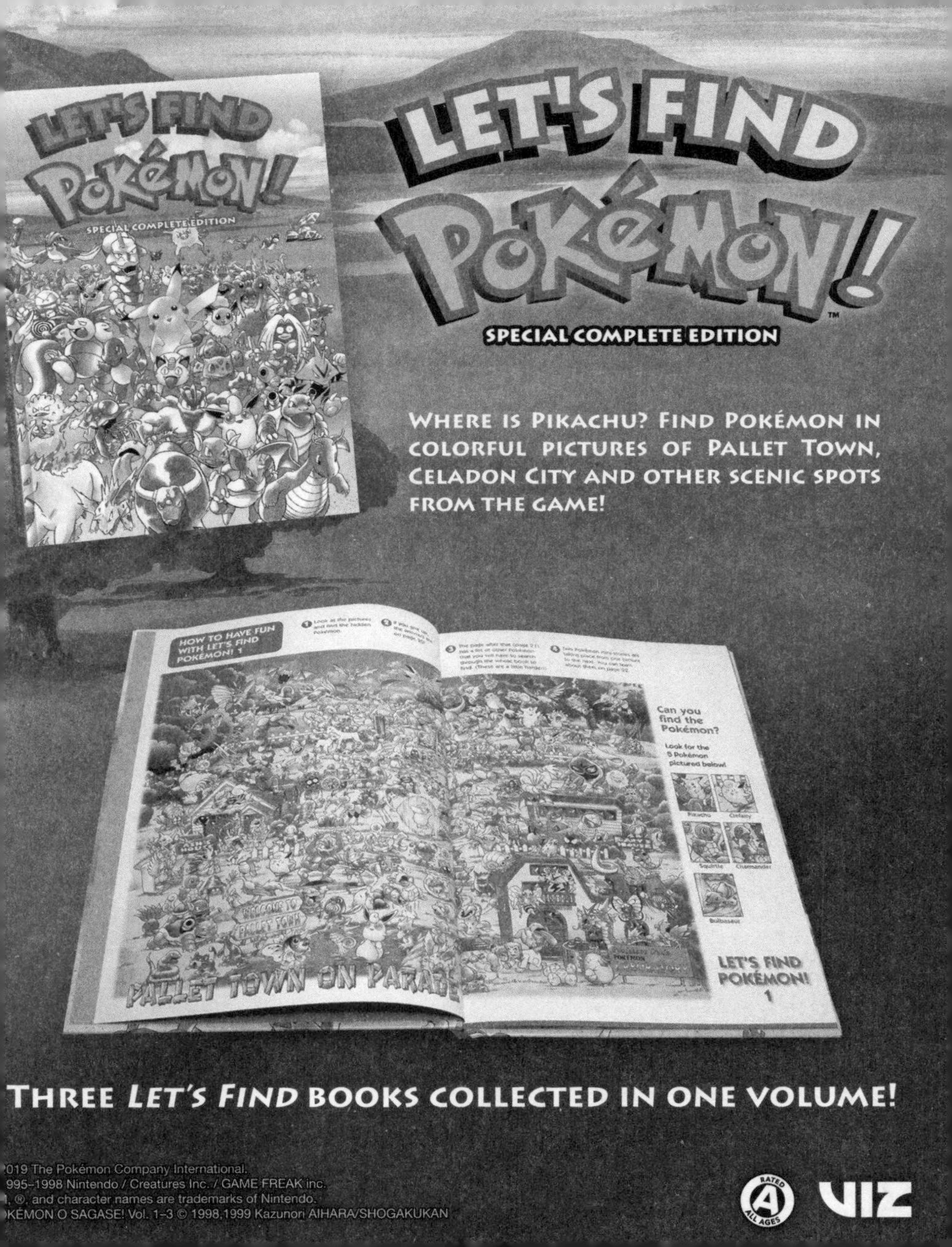
LET'S FIND POKÉMON! ™
SPECIAL COMPLETE EDITION
WHERE IS PIKACHU? FIND POKÉMON IN COLORFUL PICTURES OF PALLET TOWN, CELADON CITY AND OTHER SCENIC SPOTS FROM THE GAME!
HOW TO HAVE FUN WITH LET'S FIND POKÉMON! 1
Can you find the Pokémon?
Look for the 5 Pokémon pictured below!
PALLET TOWN ON PARADE
LET'S FIND POKÉMON! 1
THREE *LET'S FIND* BOOKS COLLECTED IN ONE VOLUME!
019 The Pokémon Company International.
995–1998 Nintendo / Creatures Inc. / GAME FREAK inc.
, ®, and character names are trademarks of Nintendo.
KÉMON O SAGASE! Vol. 1–3 © 1998,1999 Kazunori AIHARA/SHOGAKUKAN
RATED A ALL AGES
VIZ

THE ART OF

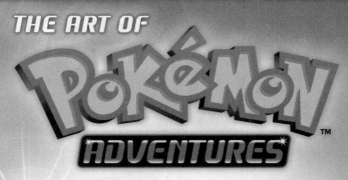

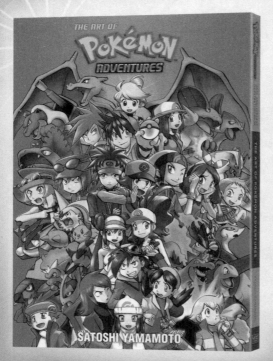

STORY AND ART BY
Satoshi Yamamoto

A collection of beautiful full-color art from the artist of the Pokémon Adventures graphic novel series! In addition to illustrations of your favorite Pokémon, this vibrant volume includes exclusive sketches and storyboards, four pull-out posters, and an exclusive manga side story!

viz.com

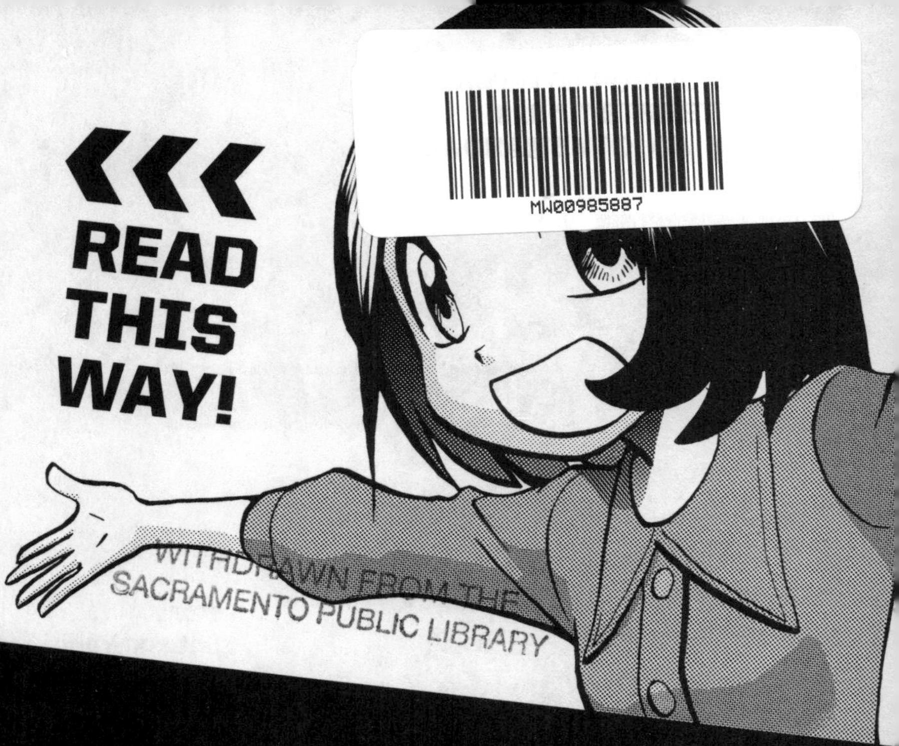
READ THIS WAY!

THIS IS THE END OF THIS GRAPHIC NOVEL!

To properly enjoy this VIZ Media graphic novel, please turn it around and begin reading from right to left.

This book has been printed in the original Japanese format in order to preserve the orientation of the original artwork. Have fun with it!

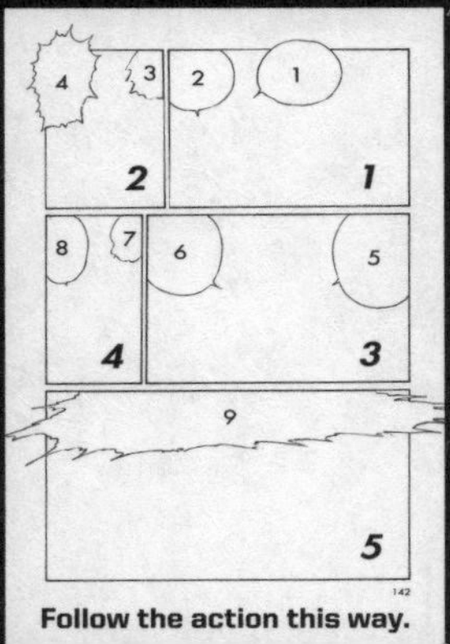

Follow the action this way.